Trouble Under the Tree

Heather Webber

Other books by Heather Webber:

The Nina Quinn Mystery Series
A Hoe Lot of Trouble
Trouble in Spades
Digging up Trouble
Trouble in Bloom
Weeding out Trouble
Trouble Under the Tree

The Lucy Valentine Novels
Truly, Madly
Deeply, Desperately
Absolutely, Positively
Perfectly Matched

The Wishcraft Mystery Series
(written as Heather Blake)
It Takes a Witch
A Witch Before Dying

Trouble Under the Tree

ISBN: 1477607560

ISBN-13: 978-1477607565

Chapter One

Thou, Nina Colette Ceceri Quinn, shall never again get caught standing beneath the mistletoe by a sneaky old man.

"Pucker up, Miz Quinn." My elderly neighbor pursed his lips like a puffer fish and made kissy noises. His white hair was slicked back with the Dax pomade he'd used for decades, and he smelled as though he'd bathed in Aqua Velva, which he'd kept stockpiled in his linen closet since 1966. He was a vintage kind of guy.

Reluctantly, I leaned in, offering him my cheek. I had my standards, and getting kissed on the lips by Donatelli Cabrera might send me into a catatonic state clear through New Year's. "You're not just trying to make Brickhouse jealous, are you?"

Ursula "Brickhouse" Krauss was a lot of things to me. Once, she'd been my evil tenth grade English Lit teacher, then she'd been a client, and now she was a part-time worker of mine—and dare I say it?—a friend.

He huffed. He puffed. He pouted. "I'm over her."

This was why I loved playing poker with Mr. Cabrera. He was a lousy liar. "You miss her."

Currently, their on-off relationship was off. Way, way off. Mr. Cabrera had the unfortunate habit of dating women who would become suddenly unavailable. As in really unavailable.

As in dead.

Rumor in the Gossip Mill (affectionately known as the Mill), the nickname of the neighborhood where we lived in Freedom, Ohio, was that Mr. Cabrera was cursed.

I knew the rumors to be true. I'd been to more funerals for his girlfriends over the years than I cared to admit.

Brickhouse and Mr. Cabrera might actually be perfect for each other, but Brickhouse, out of self-preservation, kept "taking breaks" from him every few months to increase her odds of making it to her next birthday. This recent breakup came on the heels of Brickhouse suffering a bout of the flu shortly after Thanksgiving that eventually sent her to the hospital with pneumonia (again—it was the second time this year). When Mr. Cabrera visited her in the hospital with a bouquet of flowers, he may as well been the Grim Reaper waving his scythe.

She'd sent him packing.

He'd been moping ever since.

"I don't miss her," he insisted, lying through his dentures. He adjusted the collar of his Christmas-tree emblazoned sweater. The lights on the animated fabric tree flashed brightly.

I nudged him with my elbow. "She'll come around. You know, once she's off the antibiotics."

He threw a mournful look over his shoulder, into my living room. Brickhouse stood next to the fireplace, warming her hands as she chatted with Tam Oliver, my (indispensible) personal Girl Friday at Taken by Surprise, Garden Designs, my landscaping company.

Brickhouse still didn't look too well. Pale and wan, she'd lost a good twenty pounds which made her square-shape more pear-like. Even her short spiky white hair had wilted a bit.

It was a little over a week until Christmas and my open house holiday party was in full swing, however I noticed no one else was foolish enough to hang out near the mistletoe. I couldn't blame them, with Mr. Cabrera still lurking nearby.

That was me. Nina Colette Slow Learner Ceceri Quinn.

"Well, I ain't waiting around for her," he declared. "I'm done with her calling all the shots. I deserve better than that, don't I?"

I thought Brickhouse might deserve a long life, but didn't say so. Plus, he kind of had a point. "Do you already have a new girlfriend?"

Eagerly, he rubbed his hands together. "I surely do."

These were the days of my life.

Between Mr. Cabrera's love life, my own love life, my crazy dysfunctional family, and all those murders I'd been mixed up in...I was living a daytime drama.

"Really?" I mentally prepped a warning for the poor, misfortunate woman.

His unruly white eyebrows dipped at my tone. "I'm a catch."

A catch someone would do best to toss back. I couldn't help but smile. "Of course you are."

He puffed out his barrel chest. "I asked Fairlane McCorkle to accompany me to the tree-lighting at Christmastowne tomorrow."

Christmastowne was an enormous indoor Christmas village, owned by old high school friends of mine. As a favor to them, I'd taken on the job of decking

Christmastowne's halls and had been working there for the past two weeks during its "soft open." After the grand opening, slated for tomorrow afternoon, I could go back to focusing my attentions on my one-day garden makeovers. These multiweek gigs took their toll, especially when everything that could go wrong had.

"And what did Fairlane say?" I glanced around for her. She was here somewhere—I could hear her laugh rise above the murmured conversations. Never had she struck me as a woman who had a death wish, but my perceptions and intuitions about people had been knocked off-kilter by all those murder investigations I'd been involved in.

Fairlane was fairly new to the neighborhood, considering most of its residents (aside from me) had lived here for decades. She and her twin sister, Fairlee (known as "Lele"), had moved in six months ago, which was more than long enough to have heard the Mr. Cabrera rumors—and see the curse at work firsthand (may Boom-Boom Vhrooman rest in peace). Fairlane was a vivacious lady, full of life and more than a little full of herself. Though she tended to rub me the wrong way, I really didn't want to see her get hurt. Not by a curse. And not by a rebound relationship with our resident Romeo.

"She said she'd love to," he said with a bit of braggadocio in his voice.

Assessing him carefully, I narrowed my eyes. "Are you sure you aren't using her to make Brickhouse jealous?"

"No, but it would be an added bonus." He cackled as he walked off.

I stepped far away from the mistletoe and went in search of a cup of eggnog, which I intended to spike. Heavily. I found Kit Pipe manning the bowl, looking out of place among all the frou-frou Christmas decorations my mother had insisted on putting up.

He handed me a glass of eggnog. A crystal glass—also a result of my mother's party planning. My request to use cute snowman-decorated paper cups and plates had gone out the window with my "tacky" colored Christmas lights (which would go right back up when everyone left). When Celeste Madeline Chambeau Ceceri made a decision, it was best to go with it rather than deal with the dramatic repercussions.

Besides, I'd asked for her help (what had I been thinking?), so I really only had myself to blame. "Thanks," I said, heading for the hard liquor on the counter. I poured a healthy dose of rum into my glass. "Want some?"

He pulled a flask from his front pocket. "Been there, done that."

"Smart man."

"Goes without saying."

I smiled and raised my glass in a toast to him. Kit had worked for me a long time now—he'd been my very first employee when I started my original landscaping company, which eventually morphed into TBS—a company that specialized in surprise garden makeovers completed in one day. Over the years, he'd become more than just an employee—he had become a close friend and recently, a roommate. If his relationship with my cousin Ana Bertoli continued on its hot and heavy path, he might soon be family. I couldn't be happier about that. He's a good guy, despite the fact that he looked like a complete thug. Six-five, two hundred and fifty pounds of solid muscle and multiple tattoos—including inked eyeliner and a skull on his bald head. During this past summer, he went through a stretch when he had grown out his hair, and it had been just plain strange to look at him. People usually gave him a wide berth—which was just the way he liked it.

"Where's Ana?" I asked.

"Working late."

Ana was a probation officer for the county court system. It was through her that I'd met Kit—and Tam Oliver, too. All my employees had been sent to me through Ana's job. She occasionally helped her favorite probationers find employment. TBS was the first stop on her list, since she knew I was a sucker for giving people a second chance.

It was odd for Ana to be working so late on a Friday night, and I hoped she wasn't plotting for me to hire someone else. My staff was at capacity. Winter at a landscaping company was not a time to take on a new employee. As it was, I had been lucky to keep my staff at full-time status. We had been busier this season than usual with the sudden popularity of indoor gardens, but it was the enormous job at Christmastowne that had been our saving grace. With that payday, I wouldn't have to worry about payroll through the winter months. For that security alone, it had been worth it to bend TBS's one-day only rules and take the two-week-long job.

As I added another splash of rum to my eggnog, I glanced out the kitchen window. Cars were parked in the driveway, two by two, and lined along both sides of the street. Several of the cars had antlers sticking from the windows and red noses on the grills. I smiled. Some people hated the look, but personally, I found it adorable. Not adorable enough to put on the company truck I drove around, however. I had to keep up some sense of decorum after all. I was a successful businesswoman. There were false pretenses to keep up.

Ah, screw it. I made a mental note to get myself some of those antlers tomorrow at Christmastowne.

My gaze skipped across the street to Bobby MacKenna's house. He was out of town—and had been for two weeks—which put *our* hot and heavy on hold. Indefinite hold.

I'd agreed to marry him on Thanksgiving Day.

But had been having second thoughts recently.

Partly because I wasn't entirely sure—despite trying to convince myself otherwise—that I was over my ex. We'd only split seven months ago. A lot had happened in that time. Especially a lot of forgiveness.

But mostly because Bobby and I didn't do well as a long-distance couple. Been there, done that as Kit would say. It hadn't gone well.

I caught my reflection in the glass and tried not to frown. Oh, not at my bobbed brown hair (which looked pretty good thanks to my friend Perry, a hairstylist), or my plain ol' muddy green eyes—but at the *look* in my eyes.

I looked like Mr. Cabrera.

Moping.

Egads.

I forced a brighter expression, but it just looked phony.

I sighed.

"When's Bobby due back?" Kit asked, coming up next to me.

"Not sure. His mom's heart surgery is scheduled for Monday."

Two weeks ago, Bobby had packed a suitcase, his laptop, and his grandfather Mac, and had flown to Texas, where he'd grown up, to take care of his mom. She'd started having heart trouble a few weeks ago, and when things had taken a turn for the worse it was decided she needed surgery. Since Bobby had recently quit his job to write full-time, he'd been able to drop everything to take care of her. Bobby said he'd taken Mac with him for moral support, but I think it was more because Mac couldn't be left without adult supervision for too long.

Otherwise, Mac might end up in jail again.

He had the worst habit of taking things that didn't belong to him.

"It was nice of him to let me stay at his place while he's away," Kit said.

Bobby offered Kit free rent in lieu of house-sitting. Until then, Kit had been living here with me after going through a terrible breakup with his girlfriend, who'd later been found murdered.

I winced at the memories. It had been a horrible time. Kit had been missing, and the police thought he was guilty. I shook my head, not allowing myself to go there. "He's a nice guy," I finally said.

"You hanging in?" Kit asked, his lined eyes probing.

"Yep. It's just strange not having him here." Bobby and I had been through thick and thin, including those pesky murders, my ex, and well, my crazy family and neighbors. If he could put up with all that, I could certainly deal with him being out of town for a while. After all, he was an only child. His mom needed him.

Indefinitely.

Just the thought of being alone with *my* mom indefinitely caused me to shudder. Which made me feel like an awful daughter, so I automatically forgave the crystal glasses. And the mistletoe. And the plain white lights. It was a lot of guilt I was feeling, obviously.

My guilt-o-meter was working overtime right now. It was because of the time of year—the holidays—and the fact that this would be the first Christmas in a very long time that Riley, my almost sixteen-year-old stepson, wouldn't be celebrating with me.

He'd recently decided to move in with his dad, my ex Kevin, and as a stepmom I really had no say in the matter. I dutifully ignored the tug on my heartstrings. There wasn't enough rum in the bottle to help me deal with those feelings.

Riley sulked into the kitchen, went to the fridge, and pulled out a Mountain Dew.

Speak of the devil.

"How's my favorite elf?" I asked, unable to stop a smile.

He groaned.

"Elf?" Kit asked.

"Riley got a job at Christmastowne as one of Santa's elves," I explained. "He started today."

Riley hung his head in mock shame.

Kit threw his head back and laughed, a deep rumbling that had the crystal glasses humming. He wiped tears from his eyes and barked out, "How did I miss this?"

Ry popped the top on the can of soda. "Because I took great pains to avoid everyone who might recognize me."

Kit laughed harder. "Why take the job in the first place?"

"To work on my self-esteem obviously," Riley smart-mouthed then frowned. "I need the money to buy my own wheels once I get my license."

"Dude," Kit said, "you could have asked me for a loan."

"Really?" Riley asked, blue eyes hopeful.

"No."

Riley groaned.

Kit said, "Not until after I get to see you dressed as an elf. Do you have to wear the shoes, too?" Kit made a curly motion toward his feet.

Riley had the whole outfit from elf ears to jingle hat and striped tights. Kit was going to be beside himself when he got a look at it—and I knew without a doubt he was going to go looking.

When Riley refused to answer, Kit laughed harder.

"It's not funny," Riley said and walked away.

"No one likes an angry elf," Kit called after him.

Riley muttered something under his breath, and I was pretty sure I didn't want to know what.

A flushed Fairlane caught Riley under the mistletoe. It just wasn't the poor kid's day. He leaned down and let her kiss his cheek, then headed straight for the stairs and his old bedroom, presumably for some peace and quiet. I couldn't blame him a bit.

"He's such a good boy, Nina," Fairlane cooed. "A good boy."

He had his moments, but overall he was a great kid.

She fanned her face as Kit handed her a glass of eggnog.

Fairlane was a sight. Her exact age was a mystery thanks to the plastic surgery she'd had, but I pegged her to be somewhere near sixty. With her Tweety Bird blond hair teased into an updo, lots of makeup, and skin tight clothes that showed every curve and dimple of her body, she looked like a middle-aged strumpet. Curvy in all the right places, she was a good two to three inches shorter than my five-foot-four—her head only came up to Kit's armpit while mine reached his collarbone.

She eyed him like he was a big ol' candy cane. "Thank you, honey. Aren't you a looker? Do you enjoy the company of older women?"

Kit's somewhat frightened gaze cut to me.

I nearly choked on my eggnog. "Fairlane," I said, "what would Mr. Cabrera say?"

"Donatelli? Darlin', why would he care?"

"I thought you had a date with him tomorrow?"

Her eyebrows dipped as far as the artificial filler in her face would let them. "A date?"

Maybe he had gotten the twins confused. They were identical in looks, after all, right down to their immovable foreheads. But even though they looked alike, their personalities couldn't be more different. Lele was quiet and shy—even now she stood in the corner of the living room by herself—while Fairlane was the life of the party. "To the tree-lighting ceremony at Christmastowne?"

"Oh, dear! I think there's been some confusion. I told the sweet old man I'd be there, but I'll be working."

The sweet old man. Ouch. I hoped Mr. Cabrera wasn't eavesdropping.

To Kit, she said, "Lele and I were hired to take turns manning the magic reindeer food kiosk and playing Mrs. Claus. Haven't you seen us there?"

"No," he said, obviously lying.

It was hard to miss Fairlane anywhere.

"Well, tomorrow's *my* day to be Santa's favorite lady." She put her hands on her curvy hips and swung them left and right. "Maybe you should come by and jingle my bells."

I nearly choked on my eggnog again and realized I'd suddenly gone from worrying about Fairlane to worrying about Mr. Cabrera. He didn't take rejection well. I saved Kit (whose eyes bulged dangerously) from answering by saying, "I'm not sure Mr. Cabrera realizes you'll be working."

"I suppose I should set him straight," she murmured, casting longing looks at Kit.

He nodded vigorously. "Right now."

"You're right, honey." She patted his muscled arm, her eyes going round with appreciation. "I'll be right back."

"Take your time," I called after her. To Kit, I said, "Ana would rip her hair out."

Kit grinned. "I'm used to women fighting over me. Happens all the time."

"Sure it does."

I went for more rum. I was going to regret it in the morning, but right now I didn't care.

"What's a guy got to do to get a kiss around here?" a voice said from the kitchen doorway.

My head snapped up. "I thought you said you couldn't make it tonight?"

"I never could resist a little mistletoe." Kevin Quinn, Riley's dad (and my ex-husband), made smooching noises in my direction.

I hoped and prayed Fairlane would happen by and grab him. He deserved it.

"Keep dreaming," I said.

He laughed. "I brought you this," he said, thrusting a holly plant at me.

This was just like Kevin. I hated holly. Ever since I was six and my brother Peter convinced me that its berries were delicious. I was sick for days. He was lucky I ever forgave him.

"You know I don't like holly bushes," I accused. Kevin and I had been married for seven years before splitting last May. Every year of which I told him that holly story.

"Oh." He blinked not-so-innocent green eyes. "You don't? Oops."

And this was one of the many reasons we were divorced. I set the plant on the counter. "Really," I said. "What are you doing here?"

"Riley called."

"He did?"

Even though Riley lived with his dad now, he still spent every other weekend with me. And this was one of those weekends. I tried not to feel hurt. "Does he want to go home already?"

"No, not at all," Kevin said, reading me perfectly. "He said he wanted to talk to me about Christmastowne." The lines on his forehead dipped. "About something weird going on there?"

"Weird how?" Strange things had been happening there. The fire alarm sounding every couple of hours, keys missing, power outages, refrigerators unplugged at the food court so all the food spoiled, sand sprinkled on the ice skating rink... Which did he refer to?

Shrugging, Kevin said, "Haven't got the scoop yet." He looked around. "Where is Ry?"

"Upstairs," I murmured and he turned and threaded through the crowd.

Weird. I wondered what Riley had noticed that he'd want to talk to his dad, a homicide detective, about.

It had me worried.

Kit unscrewed his flask and poured a little of the liquid into my cup. "Stop worrying so much."

"You think you know me so well."

"I do." He poured in a little more of the liquor. "Drink. That whole place is freaking weird. Christmas all year? Those people should be committed."

I smiled and sipped my drink. At this point it was more rum than eggnog. Old high school friends Jenny and Benny Christmas (honest-to-goodness, those are their real names) had sunk their life savings into opening Christmastowne, an indoor, year-round Christmas village. It was supposed to have opened in early November, but it had been plagued by delays. It finally opened its doors two weeks ago, a soft open to work out any kinks, but the kinks kept on coming.

With the grand opening tomorrow, the place was bound to be packed. Benny, a former pro football player, had called in favors from local sports celebrities who promised to make appearances. There was going to be plenty of media coverage, prize giveaways, and the lighting of the thirty-foot-tall live Christmas tree.

Jenny and Benny had hired me to deck the halls. And even though it wasn't a job I would normally take on, the money was too good to pass up. Plus, they were old friends. How could I say no? Taken by Surprise only had a few last minute touches before the village opened its doors tomorrow morning.

"I just hope there's no more trouble brewing," I said.

But unfortunately, I was suddenly feeling that something was bound to go wrong.

Horribly wrong.

Chapter Two

If I never planted another poinsettia again in my life, it would be too soon.

Slowly, I rose from my kneeling position and took off my gloves. I looked around in wonder. Christmastowne was a sight to behold. Jenny and Benny had done the impossible. They'd created an enormous retail space—three floors of shops and restaurants—without sacrificing the cozy warmth and spirit of Christmas. The halls were decked with boughs of holly (including sprigs from the plant Kevin had given me) and twinkling lights, soft carols played, and the scent of fir, peppermint, and gingerbread mingled in the air.

It should have been too much. Christmas overload. But somehow it wasn't. It felt magical.

In the grand atrium, I backed up to get a better look at the tree in all its glory and almost knocked over a toy donation bin. I set it right and looked upward. The spruce was a live tree and stood thirty feet tall. The floor around the tree had been specially crafted to be removed in a few years when the tree grew too large for the building. An intricate watering system was in place as well. It had been an incredible design feat by landscaping engineers and architects to get it done.

Above the tree was a glass snow globe-type dome that gave the tree plenty of headroom and light to thrive. The dome's construction was one of the main reasons the opening of Christmastowne had been delayed—it had been a snowy year, especially for this part of Ohio.

"It looks lovely, Nina. What a wonderful job you did."

I turned and found Jenny Christmas at my side. "The whole place is gorgeous."

Jenny and I had been friends all through high school at St. Valentine's, mostly because our names put her alphabetically behind me in homeroom, hers being Chester and mine being Ceceri. Somewhere during junior year, she'd started paying more attention to who was behind *her*, football star Benjamin (Benny) Christmas, than me. Later that year, he'd asked her to prom and they've been together ever since. She'd followed him to Ohio State where he'd been chosen for the All-America team twice, through the draft process, and finally into the NFL, where he played for the hometown Bengals. When a car accident that broke nearly every bone in Benny's body ended his career two years ago, they decided it was time to follow Jenny's dream—ever since she met Benny she'd wanted to open a retail Christmas village one day. They used his accident settlement as startup money and Christmastowne was born.

Her bright blue eyes glistened. "It's been a dream come true."

I looked around, soaked in the atmosphere. "I have a feeling this place is going to be very successful."

She linked arms with me. "From your mouth..."

Her dark hair cascaded down her back in waves, and I was happy to note that she didn't have Mr. Cabrera's taste in Christmas fashion. She wore a deep green v-necked wrap dress that cinched her tiny waist for today's big celebration.

"Are you nervous?" I asked.

"I'm just glad all the little bugs have been worked out. I swear if one more thing went wrong, I would think this place was cursed."

Personally, I thought it might be, even *if* one more thing didn't go wrong. I wanted to ask if she'd ever looked into the history of the land the building sat on. If it had been a sacred burial ground at some point—or something along those cursed lines—but I didn't think now was the best time to approach that subject.

Beneath heavily layered makeup, I could see her anxiety in the unsuccessfully hidden dark circles and the lines creasing her eyes. In the past few weeks, she looked to have aged ten years.

"Everything will work out just—"

My voice was cut off by the shrieking fire alarm. Sniffing, I picked up another scent in the air. Something burning.

"Oh no," Jenny mumbled. "Not again. Glory Vonderberg might be the best gingerbread artist in the Midwest, but she has the worst memory. She keeps putting gingerbread in the oven and forgetting to take it out. This is the third time she set off the fire alarms this week."

Ah. So that explained the fire alarms going off.

Jenny grabbed my arm. "Come with me, Nina. I might need someone to hold me back when I talk to her." Gazing deeply into my eyes, she said, "Seriously. Can you do that?"

"Hold you back?"

She nodded, her eyes filled with intensity.

"I think I can manage." I was fairly sure I'd lifted bags of mulch heavier than her. She was a tiny thing, maybe one hundred pounds. Wet. If that.

I followed her upstairs, her stilettos clicking on the curved faux-stone tiled stairs. I'd met Glory a few times already, and my first impression of her was that she was a complete ditz. It had been my second and third impressions as well.

As we passed the Magic Reindeer Food kiosk on the second floor, I waved to Lele McCorkle, who shyly waved back. I couldn't believe how different, personality-wise, she was from her sister.

"How come the sprinklers don't go off every time the fire alarm does?" I asked Jenny.

"Don't tell, but we had to disconnect the system because of Glory." Her cheeks reddened. "I've just about had it with her."

"Isn't that...dangerous?" Hello, understatement.

"Very," Jenny said. "It has to stop, or else I have to fire her, and I really don't want to do that. Early surveys from the soft open indicate Glory's shop is a customer favorite."

She glanced at me again, the intensity back. "You don't know how to bake gingerbread, do you?"

I shook my head. It was easier than admitting that I could, in fact, bake a mean gingerbread man, but the scent of molasses made me gag. It wasn't pretty, trust me.

She groaned.

"Have you had your blood pressure checked recently, Jenny?"

"I don't want to know, Nina. I really don't want to know." She smiled and nudged me. "You don't happen to know CPR, do you?"

Actually, I'd learned after one of my surprise makeovers had gone terribly, terribly wrong. "I do, but I don't think it will help if you have yourself a stroke."

"I'll be fine after Christmas is over and things settle into a steady rhythm around here."

I watched the way she marched and had the feeling she was deluding herself. I hadn't seen her often since graduating high school, but whenever I did, she exuded such high-intensity it was hard to be around her for any great length of time. She was the type that could find stress in any situation, whether it was running out of creamer for her coffee or a speck on her expensive shoes.

Hazy smoke filled the area in front of The Gingerbread Oven, but as soon as we reached the doorway, the fire alarms stopped blaring. Jenny stormed inside the shop. I followed, wondering just how serious she'd been about holding her back.

The Gingerbread Oven was divided into two parts. One was retail-oriented, where a shopper could buy all the supplies she needed to make a gingerbread house on her own—or purchase one ready-made (to pass off as her own—not that I'd ever done that. Not me, Nina Colette Phony-Baloney Gingerbread House Maker Ceceri Quinn). The other half of the space was set up as a demonstration kitchen. Here, shoppers (adults and kids alike) could create their own gingerbread house under Glory's expert guidance.

Benny was already in the kitchen with a fire extinguisher when we arrived. Glory stood waving her oven-mitted hands as the smoke slowly cleared. A tray of charred gingerbread men sat on one of the stainless steel counters. Poor little guys were burnt almost beyond recognition.

"I've got it under control," Benny said, putting the extinguisher down.

I didn't see any foam, so it didn't look like he had needed to use it.

"What happened? I thought you were going to set the timer from now on?" Jenny asked Glory.

Glory tittered and lifted a shoulder in a shrug. She was a tall woman, and her Marge Simpson hairdo gave her even more height. Long wild curls tilted precariously atop her head, secured with a clip that looked like it could pop off at any moment and take out a bystander's eye.

I backed up a step. I liked my eyes.

"I forgot?" she said.

Jenny scowled. "I might forget to pay you next time this happens, got it? In fact, I might forget you work here and ask security to escort you out. Get my drift?"

I was pretty sure the place had no security yet, but that was beside the point.

I'd never seen Jenny angry, but she was furious now. I stepped closer to her in case I did, in fact, have to hold her back.

Glory crossed her arms over her enormous chest. "I dare you to find someone better than me."

Okay, maybe I'd been wrong. The biggest part of her might be her ego. But she did have a point. At fifty-three, she was the best gingerbread artist within a five-hundred-mile radius. What she could do with gingerbread houses was astounding. And her cookies (maybe with the exception of the scorched little men on the table) were the best I'd ever tasted.

Jenny lunged. I made a grab for her and pulled her back. She was tiny, but strong as she struggled against me.

Glory was up for the fight. She jumped forward, her oven-mitted hands looking like boxing gloves. "You're playin' with fire, Jenny Christmas."

Benny stepped in between the two of them. "Now, now, even though I love a good cat fight, let's not get carried away, ladies."

I thought he might have a death wish.

"Obviously, you like fire," Jenny snapped back, ignoring Benny completely. She snatched a crispy gingerbread man and hurled it. It smacked Glory in the forehead just as she peeked around Benny's big form. "You like things so hot they burn!"

"*Argh!*" Glory's hands reached around Benny's back, clawing air.

"Let me go, Nina!" Jenny cried, arms flailing.

Jeez. Thank goodness for Duke, my scary personal trainer, or I might have been flat on my ass by now. "No!"

"It was an accident," Benny said loudly. "They happen."

Jenny immediately stopped struggling at the word "accident," and I imagined she was thinking of his accident—the one that nearly killed him.

Despite his injuries, Benny was as big and strong as ever. His clothes strained to fit his muscular body. He didn't seem to mind Jenny's anger—which was probably a good thing for their marriage.

I let her go.

She straightened her dress. "Fine."

Glory brushed crumbs from her face as she peered around Benny. "Fine." She smoothed back a strand of hair that had escaped from the straining clip.

"Just so long as it doesn't happen again," Jenny said, reaching out and cupping Benny's jaw. She squeezed his cheeks and narrowed her intense eyes. "I've got enough to deal with right now thanks to a drunken Santa and a horny Mrs. Claus. Get a handle on this, Benny. Hear me?" She spun around and stormed off.

I held back a smile at the Mrs. Claus comment—I recognized a reference to Fairlane when I heard one.

"Good riddance," Glory exclaimed when Jenny was out of earshot, then dumped the rest of the gingerbread men in a trash can.

Benny dragged a hand down his face. His looks hadn't changed at all since high school. Big, tall, beefy. A blond-haired, brown-eyed boy next door—but one who knew how good-looking he was and used it to his every advantage. "Glory, you've got to stop setting those alarms off. I'm reconnecting the sprinkler system this afternoon."

She lifted a thinly plucked eyebrow. "Maybe if I didn't have so many distractions."

Distractions? What distractions? "What distractions?" I asked.

They both looked at me as if wondering why I was still there.

"Never you mind, Nina. How about a cookie?" Glory plucked a frosted gingerbread man from a rack nearby.

My mouth watered, and I bit off his head (and didn't feel so much as a blip on my guilt-o-meter). "Delicious."

Glory smiled like a proud mama.

One thing Jenny said on her way out was bothering me. "Is Santa really drunk?" Was an inebriated Santa why Riley had called Kevin? After all, Riley worked closely with Santa yesterday—had he picked up on it?

Benny gave me a weak smile. "Shades of *Miracle on 34th Street*, don't you think?"

Glory tittered as if his comment was the funniest she'd ever heard.

"Why not fire him?" I asked.

"No backup. Besides, Santa is Jenny's uncle Dave. Drunk Dave as we call him in the family. If Jenny fired her aunt Olive's husband, holidays would be really awkward."

Glory tipped her head. "I thought his name was Kris Kringle?"

Oh boy. "I've got to go check on my crew and make sure everything's set for the opening."

As I walked out, I heard Glory say, "Really, isn't it Kris Kringle?"

I went in search of Riley. I wanted to find out what he had told Kevin last night. Curiosity was killing me.

Crossing over the Santa Express train tracks that circled the bottom floor of Christmastowne, I headed for Santa's Cottage. I was halfway there when my cell phone rang. I checked the readout and wavered on whether to answer.

It was my mother. Again.

It was the sixth call this morning. I'd ignored all the others—and she hadn't left any messages. There was only so far I could push my luck—ignoring a seventh call might prove hazardous to my health.

I decided to finally find out what she wanted. "Hi, Mom."

"Don't '*Hi Mom*,' me, young lady. You've been ignoring my calls."

I couldn't argue with that. I ignored her calls a lot. "I'm working."

"Something terrible has happened!"

My chest tightened. "Is Dad okay?"

"He's fine."

"Maria? Nate?" Maria was my baby sister—the drama queen of the family. Nate was her husband—they were still newlyweds.

"Fine. Just fine. Though, now that you mention it Maria has been acting strangely lately."

"Mom!"

"What, *chérie?*"

"What's so terrible?"

"Oh! I awoke to the most horrendous sight this morning."

"I'm sure Dad wouldn't appreciate you saying so."

She laughed. I loved her laugh—warm and genuine.

"Not your father, though some mornings that would be an apt description. Did I ever tell you how he sleeps with his mouth open? The drool alone would scare most wo—"

"Mom!"

"Oh. Right. It's my lawn."

"What's wrong with your lawn?"

"There's a—" she took a deep breath "—a giant inflatable snow globe out there. Snoopy, I believe. And that little bird friend of his."

"Woodstock?"

"That's him."

"Cute," I said, squinting to see if I could spot Riley among the elves in Santa's Cottage. Honestly, even up close they tended to look alike.

"Not cute! Not even close."

"Then why'd you put it out there?" I shouldn't have answered the phone. I still had a checklist of items to cross off before the doors opened at eleven. I really didn't even have the time to talk to Riley, but sometimes my nosiness got the better of me.

"I didn't. That's what I'm trying to tell you," she said with more condescension than I thought necessary. "Someone put it out there while I was sleeping."

I held in a laugh. "Who would do that?"

"As if I would know. Hooligans, no doubt. I've unplugged the thing, but I don't know what to do with it. It. Has. To. Go."

Ah. The real reason she called. She needed my truck.

"I'll take it." I'd always had a fondness for that cute little Woodstock.

"You do not need another lawn decoration. Perhaps you can donate it."

"There's always room for more," I said.

"Whose child are you?"

"I ask myself that often."

"Fresh."

"I'll be over after the big tree-lighting."

"What do I do with it until then? I can't leave it out there on the lawn. The neighbors might see."

"They probably already saw it."

"Lord have mercy," she murmured. "How am I going to explain?"

I laughed. "Have Dad drag it into the garage. I'll be there soon."

Before she could sneak in another word, I hung up and walked over to Santa's Cottage. Here, Jenny's ingenuity really came to life. She literally had a cottage built inside Christmastowne. It was a small one-story cabin, decked out in Christmas lights, faux snow, and even faux smoke coming out of the faux chimney. It was absolutely adorable.

Outside the cottage, a small picket fence cordoned off the area and also provided a queue for eager little kids waiting their turn to see the big guy. There was a reindeer pen off to one side, and Jenny was still trying to get real reindeer to put in it for a petting zoo along with a few other barnyard animals.

A copse of faux snow-dusted pine trees, holly bushes, and dozens and dozens of (kill me now) poinsettias added a nice touch of outdoors. Through a snow-crusted picture window, I caught a glimpse of Santa's big velvet chair— which was empty.

During the off-season Jenny planned to turn the space into Santa's workshop and have Santa hang around all year long so kids would still be eager to come to the village to get a peek at the toys he was making. It was genius.

I followed the empty queue to the open front door of the cottage. I peeked in and saw Nancy Davidson, Christmastowne's photographer, fussing with her camera equipment, which was set up next to a fireplace that had stockings hung (embroidered with "Mr. Claus" and "Mrs. Claus") by the faux fire with care. Riley stood next to a toy chest—another of Jenny's brilliant ideas. Families who wanted their pictures taken with Santa could spend a fortune on the photos—or they could drop an unwrapped present into the chest and have the shot for free. The toys were then donated to a local children's charity.

Even though most of the donated presents cost more than the picture fee it fostered the spirit of giving, and Riley commented this morning that people had responded enthusiastically. He had to empty the toy chest hourly to keep up with the flow.

Across the room, I noticed Jenny had taken a wobbly Santa aside and was giving him a talking-to. Mrs. Claus, dressed in a pretty red dress with green sash, gray curly wig, cute hat and sensible red pumps, had latched onto a poor male elf. Her hand encircled his arm, and she cooed appreciatively over his muscles.

Nancy headed toward me, and I moved out of the doorway to let her pass.

"Thanks," she said. "I had to get some fresh air. The fumes..." She fanned her face.

"What fumes?" Had there been *another* mishap?

"Like Santa has been swimming in a vat of whiskey. My eyes are watering."

"That bad?" I asked, peeking over her shoulder as Jenny's face turned redder and redder during her lecture. Hopefully she wouldn't attack her uncle the way she'd gone after Glory.

"Worse, Nina. *Blech*. Prepare yourself."

I'd come to know a lot of the employees here over the past two weeks. Nancy was older, maybe mid-fifties, with brown hair that looked streaked from natural sun, and kind, wise bright blue eyes. She'd taken this job part-time to supplement running her dairy goat farm—freelance photography was her hobby.

Holding up her camera, she said, "I'm going to take some snapshots. I'll see you later."

I supposed Santa couldn't smell much worse than I had last night after too many spiked eggnogs, so I ventured inside after Nancy headed off toward the atrium.

I took a gleeful moment to absorb the picture that was Riley. Almost six feet tall, he wore green- and red-striped tights, a velvet green tunic, a green and red Santa-style hat with attached pointy elf ears, and green booties with jingle bells and curled-up toes. It was almost too much for me for me to handle—I wanted to roll with laughter. But I managed to keep a (somewhat) straight face as I walked over to him. He, on the other hand, grinned from ear to pointy ear. "What's so funny?" I asked.

"Just enjoying the show."

"What show?"

He nodded toward Mrs. Claus. Fairlane had pressed her impressive chest against the elf. Poor guy. It was blatant sexual harassment if I ever saw it. "That's really not funny," I said. "I'm embarrassed for her."

Riley looked down at me (I really hated that his growth spurt now had him a good six inches taller). "Well, I'm amused."

I was about to give him a lecture when I took a good look at the elf. Suddenly, I was amused, too.

The elf was Kevin.

Chapter Three

After Kevin extricated himself from Fairlane's iron grasp, he tried to sneak out the back door of the cottage without my noticing.

I was hip to his tactics, though, and went out the front and circled around. I came face to face with his elfish self near the faux stone chimney.

"I don't know where to begin," I said.

The bells on his sleeve jingled when he folded his arms across his chest. "You can stop grinning like that, for one."

"I can't help it. There are just some memories I want imprinted on my brain forever. This is one of them. I wish I had my camera. I could use this image on my Christmas cards. I wonder if Nancy would be willing to—"

"Stop. Stop it right now."

My smile stretched so wide it hurt my cheeks. "Unless you want this—" I gestured to his outfit "—sent to one hundred of our nearest and dearest, I suggest you tell me what you're doing here. Dressed like that?"

"Stooping to blackmail, Nina?"

"It's not the first time."

He rolled his eyes, took my elbow, and pulled me toward the pine trees. "I'm kind of working."

"Kind of?" He was a homicide detective, and unless there was a body hidden in Santa's toy chest, I was pretty sure there hadn't been a murder. News like that was sure to get around.

"Remember how Riley wanted to talk to me last night?"

How could I forget? I was dying to know why. "Yeah?"

Kevin glanced left, then right. "He thinks someone is stealing the toys from the donation chest and asked for my help. I talked to Jenny this morning, and she agreed to let me work here unofficially for a few days to see what I can find out."

A few days of Kevin in an elf outfit. This was a present that was going to keep on giving. Even though I was done with Christmastowne after this afternoon, I was going to have to come back.

With a camera.

"Why does Ry think someone's stealing?" I asked.

"One of his jobs yesterday was to empty the toy chest that's inside Santa's Cottage. He saw toys go in, like Game Boy games and those dolls everyone's so crazy about this year, but when he emptied the chest, those toys were gone. He's afraid that because he's in charge of the toys, someone is going to think he's stealing them."

I was outraged on his behalf. "That's crazy."

"You know that. I know that. But someone else might be trying to frame him."

"Well, we have to figure out who and stop them."

It was his turn to grin. "*I* have to figure out who." Placing strong hands on my shoulders, he spun me around. "*You* have to leave now."

"Hey!"

He brushed against the tree and glittery snow sprinkled onto his shoulders. "You being over here is only going to call more attention to me. I'm trying to blend in."

I laughed. "Yeah, because a tall, dark, handsome, sparkly elf is the norm around these parts."

His eyebrows waggled. "Handsome?"

"Get over yourself."

"You're the one who said it."

"I'm leaving now."

"It's about time."

Shaking my head, I turned and headed toward the atrium. Kevin was on my heels (I was pretty sure he wanted see for himself that I really left) as Fairlane came running out of the cottage, nearly knocking us both down.

Her Mrs. Claus wig was askew as Kevin reached out to steady her. Tears streamed down her face in dark rivulets. Mucus dripped from her nose.

"What's wrong, Fairlane?" I asked.

"I—I've been fired!" she wailed.

"Why?" Kevin asked.

I had a fairly good idea.

Using her sleeve, she wiped her nose. "An incident between me and Mr. Claus, is all. Jenny misunderstood."

"Did that incident have anything to do with you touching him inappropriately?" I asked. Hey, it seemed like a reasonable question to me.

She stomped her foot. "We were under the mistletoe! And it was consenting, I might add."

"Isn't Santa married?" Benny had said something about Santa being married to Jenny's aunt.

Fairlane waved a dismissive hand. "Hardly anyone can resist my charms. Especially under the mistletoe. I'm a fantastic kisser."

Ugh. I was starting to feel queasy.

Kevin said, "This just happened?"

"Yes. In there." Nodding, she motioned to the cottage.

His eyebrows dipped. "There's no mistletoe in there."

With cheeks bright red, she pulled a sprig from her pocket. "I might have been holding it."

"Oh, Fairlane," I said.

She wiped her nose again. I took a step away from her sleeve. Gross.

"A misunderstanding," she mumbled.

Kevin said, "Who's going to take over as Mrs. Claus?" He threw a look my way. "You might have to fill in, Nina."

"I'm not touching that costume," I said. "No offense, Fairlane."

She glanced at her snot-covered sleeve and looked sheepish. "There is another costume, but you don't have to worry. Lele will take over." Watery eyes blinked, and Fairlane's lips curved into a tremulous pout. "I can't believe Jenny fired me." Fairlane tipped her head. "I'm a fantastic worker. A people person. People love me."

Modest, too.

"I just don't understand," she said, trying to frown but the face-filler wouldn't let her. "Lele never gets fired."

Maybe because Lele could keep her hands to herself? But there was no point in rubbing salt in Fairlane's wounds. "Something else will come along."

"There won't be a need. All I have to do is talk to Benny. He'll fix this."

I rather doubted Benny would win that argument with Jenny.

"How can you be so sure?" Kevin asked.

Batting her eyelashes, she patted her hair and realized that her wig was off-kilter. She hurriedly straightened it. "Like I said, hardly anyone can resist my charms."

I wanted to gag.

Kevin goaded her. "I can understand why."

I frowned at him—no plastic surgery for me, so he got the full effect.

He winked.

Ugh.

"I better go change and find Benny." Fairlane again batted her eyelashes at Kevin. "A hug would make me feel so much better. It's been a traumatic morning."

"Go ahead, Nina," he said, nudging me. "Hug her."

Before I could retort, Fairlane had thrown herself into his arms.

Ha! Had to love karma.

Horrified, he stood there stiffly while her hands roamed his back. "You're so strong," she cooed.

I bit back a laugh as he patted her back twice and pushed her away.

She pulled the mistletoe out and waved it above her head.

"I've got to get back inside," he said and ran for the door, jingling all the way.

Fairlane glanced at me, tucked the sprig back into her pocket, and hurried off.

I didn't take it personally.

Two hours later all the employees of Christmastowne had gathered 'round the Christmas tree in the atrium. The doors were set to open in fifteen minutes, and Jenny and Benny were giving a last minute pep-talk.

I stood off to the side with Kit and Jean-Claude Reaux, another long-time employee, who had just finished installing yew bushes in decorative planters around the food court. With that, we were done with our work at Christmastowne.

"I think Riley is avoiding me," Kit said.

"That's because you threatened to videotape him and put it on You Tube."

Jean-Claude said, "Do you think they sell those tights here? The red and green ones? With stripes?"

Kit and I looked at him. He was serious.

Pink filled his cheeks. "I'm just curious." He watched the elves for a few seconds and said, "Do they?"

"What?" I asked.

"Sell them here?"

"Probably," I said. I'd found myself a pair of antlers and a red nose for my truck. I couldn't wait to put them on it.

He nodded, his gaze hopping from one shop to the next, as if trying to figure out which one would stock the tights.

To Kit, I said, "Should I ask him why he wants them?"

"No."

That was probably wise. With Jean-Claude, sometimes denial was best. Like the time I found out he'd been working as an exotic dancer under the name JC Rock.

Kit squinted, blinked, then squinted again. "Is that Kevin?"

My ex lurked near a column, trying to blend in. As if. "If you can get a video of him, I'll give you a big Christmas bonus."

Kit whipped out his smart phone and stalked off. He stalked well for such a big guy. I was impressed.

Benny shouted, "Everyone take your places, it's time!"

Workers scattered to their shops and kiosks, while the elves and a somewhat sober-looking Santa headed to greet the guests.

At exactly eleven o'clock, Jenny opened the front doors. The elves launched into a rousing rendition of "We Wish You a Merry Christmas" as shoppers streamed inside, *ooh*ing and *ahh*ing.

Kit, I noticed, was still stalking Kevin, who was doing his best to hide.

I spotted Brickhouse Krauss and my neighbor Flash Leonard come inside, as well as a brightly-dressed Mr. Cabrera. Really, there was no missing him with his vivid red knit cardigan with galloping reindeer stitched across the chest.

Brickhouse and Flash found their way over to me, and Flash said, "What a place!"

Flash was one of my favorite people in the neighborhood. At ninety, and wracked with arthritis, he always had a smile and managed to stay active.

Even grumpy Brickhouse agreed. "It makes me want to buy something."

"And that's saying something," I said.

She gave me an evil eye—not quite as good as my mother's but close. "What are you trying to say? Are you saying I'm cheap?"

"Yes."

Her pursed lips gave way to a smile. "I prefer frugal."

"Are you feeling any better?" I asked.

"Much," she said. "I should be back to work on Tuesday."

I'd given my crew Sunday and Monday off—they deserved it. This had been a tough job. Brickhouse had started working for me part-time as my office manager a couple of months ago, sharing the job with Tam so that she could spend more time at home with baby Niki. It was a solution that had worked out quite well.

Brickhouse's face hardened, and I followed her gaze to see Mr. Cabrera standing on the other side of the atrium.

She caught my eye and clucked. "I don't miss him."

"I didn't say you did."

"You were thinking it," she said.

"Maybe," I admitted.

She folded her arms across her big chest. "Well, I don't."

"I'm glad we settled that." Shifting the conversation, I said, "What have you got there, Flash?"

He had something in his hand. Proudly, he held it up, which was quite the struggle. His arthritis made dexterity almost impossible. "One of my old baseballs."

Once upon a time, Flash had been a semi-pro pitcher. "Did you bring it to get signed today?" Benny had brought in local sports personalities, including Reds baseball players, for the opening and there were already big crowds at their booths.

"Heavens, no. Not unless there are some old-timers here! Men who truly knew how to play the game." His out-of-control bushy gray and white eyebrows rose. "I just want to show it off. They don't make balls like this anymore."

I smiled. More like he wanted to reminisce about the good ol' days with some young fellas who'd be willing to swap war stories. He headed off to stand in line.

I caught Brickhouse looking at Mr. Cabrera again.

"I don't miss him!" she insisted.

"If you say so."

She clucked and strode off.

I looked around for Jean-Claude, but he'd wandered off as well—probably to buy his coveted stockings.

Kit and Kevin were nowhere to be seen.

Benny pushed through the crowd and headed straight for me, walking pretty fast considering the limp. It was the only outward indication of his accident. "Have you seen Mrs. Claus? Fairlane?" he corrected.

"Last I saw of her, Jenny had fired her and she was going to find you to get her job back. She didn't find you I take it?"

He heaved a world-weary sigh. "No. Why did Jenny fire her?"

"I believe Fairlane might have groped Santa one too many times."

His brown eyes widened then he asked, "When was this?"

"About an hour and a half ago. But Lele was supposed to be filling in as Mrs. Claus. She should be around here somewhere."

"Well, she's not," he said. "And now I don't have a Mrs. Claus." He sized me up.

"Don't even think about it."

He frowned and limped off.

Ten minutes later, he and Jenny made a welcome announcement and started counting down the Christmas tree lighting.

I grabbed a good spot by the low granite wall that circled wide around the spruce. The wall had been put in place to keep people from getting too close—and hopefully discourage kids from trying to climb the tree. A giant custom-made Christmas tree skirt blanketed the space beneath the tree, and large empty boxes that had been fancily-wrapped like presents dotted the skirt.

Across from me, Nancy Davidson snapped pictures of the crowd. Newspaper photographers also took plenty of shots. Flashbulbs flickered all around me. The excitement in the room was palpable.

Someone bumped into me, and I turned and found Flash scowling. "Dang whippersnappers didn't even know who Bobo Newsom was."

I was afraid to admit that I didn't either.

"Ten, nine, eight," Jenny called out.

"I'm sorry." I patted his hand and the baseball he held loosely popped out and rolled toward the tree. Flash started after it.

I held him back. "You can't go in there."

"Six, five, four," Benny said.

"I dare you to stop me, young lady. That there's my ball, and I mean to get it back."

"Two, one!" Benny made a grand show of flipping a giant switch.

Nothing happened.

The Christmas tree stayed dark.

The crowd booed.

I glanced over at Jenny and Benny, who both wore looks of sheer panic. Several elves hustled over to the power box and started tinkering.

Flash tried to lift his leg over the wall.

I grabbed onto him. I couldn't have him crawling under the tree. With his arthritis, it might take hours. "Wait here. I'll get it."

He patted my cheek. "You're a good girl, Nina Quinn."

"Yeah, yeah," I mumbled, sliding over the granite ledge.

The crowd's boos grew louder as I carefully crawled across the tree skirt. I hoped that if anyone saw me, they'd think I was trying to fix the lights.

I carefully avoided the large boxes. As I neared the ball, which had settled against the trunk of the tree, I scooted around one last present and stopped short when I saw a shoe laying next to the box. It was a sensible red pump.

Odd.

Then I noticed a clump of gray curls poking out from under the box as well, and I started to get a bad feeling. A very bad feeling.

I gulped and oh-so-casually lifted the box.

Oh no. Oh. No. Ohnoohnoohnoohnoohno!

"Nina!" Jenny yelled in a harsh whisper as she crawled toward me. "What are you doing?"

"We have a problem," I said, leaning back into a crouch.

"No kidding. Did you figure out what's wrong with the lights?"

"It's a bigger problem."

Impatiently, she snapped, "What could possibly be a bigger problem right now?"

My gaze met hers as she reached my side. "I found Mrs. Claus."

"Oh, thank God. Now Benny can stop freaking out. Where?" she looked around the room.

I pointed under the box.

"Why would she be in there? I can just kick myself for hiring those McCorkle sisters. Nothing but trouble. Is she sleeping?"

"Kind of," I said. "She's dead."

Chapter Four

"Dead?" Jenny gasped.

Suddenly, the tree lit up over our heads and the crowd cheered, a raucous roar. They were oblivious to the trouble brewing under the tree, which was probably a good thing.

Jenny had gone pale, and the colored lights on her face made her look polka-dotted. "Are you sure she's dead? Maybe she's just sick or something?"

"Not one hundred percent, but I've seen a few dead bodies and she looks pretty dead. The bulging eyes, the puffed out lips..."

"Oh dear God, stop. I think I'm going to be sick."

I clamped my lips together and looked around at the crowd. They'd launched into "Jingle Bells" and were swaying together like they were at a Bon Jovi concert. I expected lighters to be held up any second now.

"We need to call the police," I said. Wait. The police were here. "We need to find Kevin."

She clamped down on my arm. "Now?"

"Yes," I said slowly, drawing the word out into four syllables. "They need to know what's happened."

Jenny glanced around. "Can't we wait until later? Until after we close?"

I stared at her.

"What?" she said. "She's already dead! What's a few more hours?"

I forgave her thinking because she'd been under a lot of stress lately, but there was no way I was leaving Fairlane under that box all day.

"We have to," I said firmly, in my best stepmother tone.

"Oh my." She began to rock.

I felt movement to my left and saw Flash belly-crawling over to us, slow as an inchworm. "Nina, where's my ball?"

I reached over, grabbed the ball, and handed it to him as he wriggled up to us.

"Whatcha got there?" he asked, nodding to the box.

I was still holding the corner of it off the ground.

"A dead Mrs. Claus," I said softly, still not quite believing what I was seeing.

Jenny wailed.

Flash looked at me, gauged my sincerity, then peeked under the box. He came up shouting, "Call 9-1-1! We need an ambulance!"

He could shout amazingly loud for an old guy.

"Jingle Bells" immediately silenced, and Flash flipped the giant present over, revealing the body beneath.

Gasps went through the crowd in an echoing wave. Mothers covered their children's eyes. Gawkers moved in for a closer look.

Flash leaned over Fairlane to check for a pulse but drew his hand back. A pair of elf tights was wrapped around her throat, looking like a red- and green-striped scarf.

My stomach flipped, then flopped. For as many dead bodies as I'd seen, it never got easier. I didn't know how Kevin handled his job.

"*Ohhhh,*" Jenny moaned.

Flash reached for a wrist instead. He looked back at me, shaking his head. "She's a goner."

No kidding.

Benny jumped the knee-high wall around the tree and gimped toward us. As he neared, he stopped short, his arms wind-milling to regain his balance. His gaze immediately went to Jenny, who had squeezed her eyes shut.

"What happened?" he asked, looking between all of us, his horrified gaze landing on Mrs. Claus.

"She's a goner," Flash said again. "Dead as a doornail."

Jenny whimpered.

"I didn't know lips could turn so blue," Flash said, leaning in for a closer look.

Flashbulbs popped left and right. Reporters inched in, climbing over the wall like ants headed for a picnic.

I pulled Flash back. "Why don't you go hold off the press? Keep them as far away as you can."

His rheumy eyes lit. "Done!"

As if in slow motion, he set his prized baseball next to me, moaned as he stood up, and trundled off to the reporters. He held his arms out wide and said, "Nothing to see here, folks! Well, there is a dead body, but this is a time to honor the dead and keep back."

I groaned as a fresh wave of gasps went through the crowd. I heard rapid jingling and looked up to find Kevin running toward us. It was a sight, let me tell you, what with the cotton puff on his elf hat bobbing up and down with each step.

Benny had sat next to Jenny and gathered her in his arms. She was still moaning.

Kevin spoke into his cell phone, and when he finished the call, he looked at me and said, "Just another ordinary day on the job for you."

I shrugged. "It's really not my fault I keep finding dead bodies."

Benny's eyes widened. "How many have you found?"

"A couple," I murmured. Truth was, I might be just as cursed at Mr. Cabrera.

Oh my gosh—Mr. Cabrera.

Maybe his curse extended to *potential* girlfriends, as well. The poor guy.

I searched the crowd for my neighbor and found him not too far away, his dark eyes wide. And not two feet behind him stood Brickhouse, looking rather smug. As if saying, "I told you so." She wasn't a fool, that Brickhouse.

Kevin crouched and checked the body for a pulse as well. Then he looked at us, and said, "You need to clear this area." He muttered something about tainted evidence and stood up. Or tried to. He'd stepped on Flash's baseball, and his feet went flying out beneath him. He landed flat on his ass in a cacophony of angry jingles.

The crowd *oooh*ed.

"Don't say a word," he said to me from his prone position.

I pressed my lips together—tight— and offered him a hand up.

I couldn't help my inner glee, however, when I spotted Kit, still filming. He'd caught the fall on video. I foresaw a popcorn and movie night in my future.

Flash basked in the press limelight, answering every question thrown at him, as I followed Benny and Jenny away from the scene.

Benny had his arm around his wife, supporting her as she wobbled. I heard Jenny say to him, "There's no such thing as bad publicity, right?"

Brickhouse said, "And he keeps telling me he's not cursed." She clucked loudly enough that it echoed in the almost-empty atrium.

The police had funneled all the customers out, but wanted me to stay behind to answer a few questions.

Brickhouse, being her bossy self, had claimed she was with me, and stayed put. She liked to be in the know.

"He might be a little cursed," I said.

She gave me a dubious look. "And you might be a little nosy."

Point taken.

"To think that Benjamin Christmas asked me to be Mrs. Claus." She clucked again.

"He did?" I asked in amazement. I always thought Mrs. Krauss's face looked a lot like Mrs. Claus, but her temperament was a far cry from the benevolent character. Then again, so was Fairlane's.

"Right after I arrived here. You do not have to sound so amazed. I'd be a good Mrs. Claus."

"Yet you obviously turned down the job."

"I taught school for thirty-five years. I've had enough of whiny little kids."

"You taught high school."

"Your point being?"

I smiled.

She shivered. "It could have been me under that box. And don't you dare crack any jokes, Nina Ceceri."

Way back when, Brickhouse had been my tenth grade English teacher. We hadn't gotten along then, but these days we tolerated each other fairly well. She still liked to call me by my maiden name, though, as if chastising me in front of the whole class.

Which she had done a lot.

"He never liked me, that Benjamin Christmas." Brickhouse had also been Jenny and Benny's teacher. "Once I caught him making faces behind my back."

"Everyone made faces behind your back."

She clucked and gave me the evil eye again.

Suddenly, a scream rent the air. "Lele!"

Brickhouse and I gaped at each other as Fairlane barreled through the front doors. Two patrol officers caught her by the arms and held her back.

My gaze shifted from her to the box, back and forth.

Oh. My. It hadn't been Fairlane under there?

"Lele!" Fairlane shouted, her voice cracking.

Kevin, who'd unfortunately changed his clothes, walked over to the officers, whispered something to them, and took Fairlane's arm. She crumpled against him, putting one hand around his waist, the other on his chest, and it looked to me like her fingers were searching for nipples.

I rolled my eyes. Even in grief, she couldn't help herself.

"Hussy," Brickhouse mumbled.

I couldn't argue with that, though I didn't agree aloud because I understood the pain Fairlane must be experiencing. I could cut her some slack. For now.

"So, it was *Fairlee* under the box?" I said. Strangled. I was even more confused now. Because for as much as Fairlane wasn't likeable, Lele was. She was quiet and sweet. Who would want to kill her?

"You were never one to see the obvious," she said.

I made a face. It wasn't behind her back.

She clucked again.

"What does this mean for Mr. Cabrera's curse?" I asked Brickhouse.

"*Ach*," she said dismissively. "It doesn't change anything. Not a whit. The two sisters were practically the same person. Looks-wise, at least. What goes for one, goes for the other."

I thought she was in a bit of denial, but didn't say so.

See, I had a strong sense of self-preservation as well.

Looking around, I tried to find Riley in the employees milling about, but he was nowhere to be found. I saw Glory peering down from the second floor balcony, her hair threatening to topple over the railing. I hoped she hadn't left her gingerbread in the oven without a timer again—the last thing we needed right now was another fire alarm.

I wondered where Kit had gotten off to and finally spotted him chatting with Nancy Davidson across the atrium. She was showing him her camera, pointing out different features. Seeing them together gave me a great idea for Kit's Christmas present. A camera would be perfect for him and his newfound interest in taking pictures—and video. I made a mental note to talk to Nancy in hopes she'd have a recommendation for a good brand. Then I saw Jenny standing in a corner, looking like her world had crumbled in on her.

I supposed it had.

I told Brickhouse I'd be right back, and walked over to Jenny. Her right eye twitched as she looked at me. "How are we going to recover from this, Nina?"

"The shock will wear off," I said optimistically. "The curiosity-seekers will come in droves."

"Maybe," she said, sniffling.

Her words earlier, about there being no bad publicity wove through my thoughts. For a split second I considered she might have had something to do with the murder, but then I dismissed it.

No one could have known I'd find the body when I did. It was put under that box to be hidden—and remain that way for as long as possible.

Which had me thinking about how someone could have possibly placed a body under there with no one seeing.

Sure, we'd all been busy, but by my calculations, the murder had to have taken place between the fire alarm going off (when I'd waved to Lele at the reindeer food kiosk) and after Fairlane had been fired (because Lele had been wearing a Mrs. Claus costume). That was only a two-hour window.

"How did the police know it was Lele?" I asked.

"An officer was sent to the McCorkle house and Fairlane answered the door. It's remarkable how identical they are. Were," she clarified in a whisper.

Identical.

Brickhouse's words rang in my ears.

The two sisters were practically the same person. Looks-wise, at least. What goes for one, goes for the other.

Which suddenly had me wondering if the killer had murdered the right sister. After all, it was Fairlane who was supposed to play Mrs. Claus today, not Lele.

What if this murder had been a case of mistaken identity?

I looked over at Fairlane, who was still draped across Kevin, and thought about the repercussions if what I suspected was true.

If the killer realized the wrong sister was killed, Fairlane was in very real danger.

Grave danger.

Chapter Five

It was late afternoon by the time I pulled my truck into my mother's driveway. She was waiting for me at the front door.

"What's this I hear about a murder at Christmastowne? It's been on the news. Nina Colette Ceceri, why did I have to hear about it on the news?" she demanded, her voice rising to new decibels. "Why didn't you call me?"

"Hi, Mom." I kissed her cheek.

The house smelled of baking bread and old books—two of my favorite scents. My dad sat in his favorite recliner, reading a magazine. I gave him a kiss, too, and tousled what was left of his hair.

"Nina!" my mother stamped her foot.

"What?" I blinked innocently. It was a look I had trouble pulling off even when I was, in fact, innocent.

She let out a frustrated breath. "Do not tell me you were the one to find the body."

I sat on my dad's ottoman. "Okay."

"Neeee-na!" My mother threw her hands in the air. "What am I supposed to tell my friends who wonder why *my* daughter keeps finding dead bodies?"

"You'd prefer someone else's daughter?"

"Of course, *chérie.*"

My mother loved using the French endearment. It made her feel cultured.

A large Christmas tree stood in the corner of the room, looking majestic. It was covered in white lights, white feather garland, and delicate crystal ornaments. I knew that somewhere on the tree, probably buried deep within the boughs, was a red and green paper snowflake with elementary school pictures of Maria, Peter, and me. Maria had made it in Sunday school when she was six, and it was my father's favorite. He insisted it be hung every year (despite my mother's temper tantrums about it). It was Mom's only concession of color on the tree—and I suspected it was allowed only because my father threatened to hang his collection of Elvis ornaments (of which there were many) if she didn't comply.

Theirs was a marriage about compromise.

My father winked at me. "I think finding dead bodies is a handy talent to have. Did you know on this day in 1765, Eli Whitney was born? He invented the cotton gin, you know." He glanced at my mother. "Speaking of gin, do we have any? Nina looks like she could use a drink. Finding dead bodies must take its toll."

My mother's eyes looked ready to pop out of her perfectly coiffed head.

It reminded me a bit too much of how Lele McCorkle's eyes had looked under that box, and it made me shiver.

"Maybe a hot toddy?" my father suggested.

"Maybe a hot chocolate," I said, blinking my not-so-innocent eyes at my mother.

She narrowed hers in a perfect Ceceri Evil Eye. A double one at that. It was too much for me to resist. "Fine. While you're making the hot chocolate, I'll tell you all about my morning."

My mother said, "Now that's my good girl."

My father went back to his magazine and whispered, "Capitulator."

"Self-preservation," I countered.

"Smart girl," said my dad as I walked into the kitchen.

A loaf of freshly-baked bread sat on the counter. I eyed it. "When did you learn to make bread?" Usually, she bought the Pillsbury kind that comes in a can from the local Kroger and passed it off as her own.

"I didn't. Your sister brought it over."

I poked the loaf. "My sister Maria?"

"Do you have another?" she retorted as she chopped a square of semisweet chocolate.

"Dad could have been living a double life all these years. You never know. It could happen."

"Tee-hee," my father laughed.

My mother waved the knife. "He wouldn't dare."

My father, I noticed, still smiled. He loved getting under my mother's skin. It was his favorite pastime next to being a history and Elvis buff.

"Since when does Maria know how to bake?" Last I checked, she didn't even know how to turn on her oven.

"I told you she's acting strangely," Mom said. She poured milk into a saucepan and warmed it up.

My mother made a mean hot chocolate, but secretly, I preferred Swiss Miss. Mom's recipe was a very close second, though.

"You need to talk to her. Something is going on," she said. "Last week she called from the grocery store and asked me if I needed anything."

"Maria knows where the grocery store is?" I was only half-kidding.

Mom whisked sugar and vanilla extract into the milk. "Exactly my point."

"Maybe she's finally throwing herself into being a newlywed to impress Nate?"

"Maybe she's had a lobotomy," Mom said.

True enough. Maria rarely thought of anyone beside herself. I was going to have to check this out, because despite myself, now I was curious as to what was going on.

Mom stirred the chopped chocolate into the warm sweetened milk. Delicious scents filled the kitchen. She said, "Now tell me, did Mrs. Claus really get whacked?"

"Whacked?" I repeated.

Dad said, "Your mom has been watching *Sopranos* repeats."

She wiggled her champagne blond eyebrows. "I kind of think that Tony Soprano is handsome. Is that wrong?"

"Yes," I said. "Yes, it is."

She frowned at me.

"Turns out," I said, "that it was *Fairlee* McCorkle who was murdered. Strangled. At first we thought it had been *Fairlane*."

"Lele!" Mom said, shocked. "Why?"

"I don't know. When I left, Kevin was still interviewing employees."

"Who is twisted enough to put a body under a Christmas tree?" Mom said, whisking away. "That's just wrong. Poor Benny and Jenny," she added as she poured the liquid into mugs. "They've been through so much. First Benny's accident, now this. Has he fully recovered from that car wreck?"

"He walks with a bit of a limp," I said. "Otherwise, you would never be able to tell he'd been critically injured."

Mom *tsk*ed again. "It's a miracle he made it out alive." She made the sign of the cross even though she hadn't been to church in decades. "Unlike that poor girl who died in the crash. What was her name?"

I wracked my brain but couldn't come up with it. The crash had happened nearly two years ago in March. It had been after midnight, the road had been covered in black ice, and the two cars collided head-on.

Investigators reported that the young woman who died had crossed into Benny's lane. But reports also showed that Benny had an elevated alcohol level. Not enough to be considered legally drunk, but enough, experts said, to impair his reaction time. After the crash happened, there had been speculation the accident may have been avoided—or at the very least it would not have been as severe—if Benny had been stone-cold sober.

Jenny told me that Benny hadn't touched a drop of alcohol since, and that he was still dealing with the demons born that night. He'd even been the subject of a documentary that followed his rehabilitation. *The Recovery of an All-American Hero.* The ratings had been huge, and Benny had become a national star—bigger now than before the accident.

"Carrie Hodges," my father said.

My mother snapped her fingers. "That's it. Pretty young thing, she was. Her poor family."

Immediately, a photo of a dark-haired girl popped into my mind. It had been shown on the news and in the papers over and over. She'd been heading home from graduate school to spend spring break with her family, who lived in the area.

I dropped two peppermint marshmallows into my mug and watched them melt. It never ceased to amaze me how quickly a life could change.

My mother brought a mug out to my father and kissed the top of his head. She kissed mine on her way back as well.

Suddenly, I felt the need to wrap Riley in a bear hug.

And to call Bobby, just to hear his voice.

Mom must have been reading my mind, because she said, "Have you heard from Bobby lately?"

"He called last night. No news quite yet. He loves the weather down there. Eighty degrees and sunny."

"I'm green with envy," my mother said. "Perhaps we need a vacation, Tonio."

Dad said, "I've always wanted to visit the ruins of Machu Picchu."

"I was thinking more along the lines of a cruise in the South Pacific," Mom said lightly.

"Oh." He turned the page of his magazine and didn't say another word.

I wondered what the compromise would be on this one.

I finished my hot chocolate, and said, "I should be getting home. Where's Snoopy?"

My mother's face morphed into a scowl, and suddenly she looked like an evil queen in a storybook. "When I find out who's doing this, *ooooo!*" She shuddered with anger.

"You'll visit them with a poisoned apple?" I asked.

"What?"

"Nothing," I mumbled, heading for the door leading into the garage.

Sure enough, there was a large plastic puddle on the floor. Next to it, an air compressor.

Someone had shelled out a lot of money for this particular prank. And a suspect was forming in my mind.

"You didn't hear the air compressor running last night?" I asked.

"Thanks to the earplugs I wear to block your father's snoring, I hear very little at night."

"Dad didn't hear anything, either?"

"Are you kidding?" she asked. "Without his hearing aid in, he wouldn't hear if a plane landed in the yard."

I was suddenly glad they had a good alarm system, not that either would hear it if it went off.

I reached down to scoop up the snow globe.

"Isn't it hideous?" Mom asked.

"It's going to look perfect in my side yard."

"Where did I go wrong in raising you?" she asked.

"I think Peter dropped me on my head when I was a baby."

"That explains it."

My dad helped me load Snoopy into my truck, and I gave them both kisses and drove off.

At the end of the street, I turned left, in the opposite direction of my house.

As much as I wanted to spend some quality time with Riley watching a *Die Hard* marathon, there was someone I wanted to talk to.

I glanced back at Snoopy.

And she had better have a good alibi for last night.

She answered on the third knock, and I flashed my keychain light into her eyes. "Where were you between the hours of midnight and six a.m.?"

"Have you been hitting the leftover eggnog?" my cousin Ana Bertoli asked. She waved me inside her apartment and closed the door.

Colored Christmas lights had been tacked along the ceiling, mini Santa Clauses cluttered every surface, and a large silver tree with pink lights stood in the center of the room. Every branch had an ornament—or two—weighing it down. A giant rhinestone star topped the tree like an elaborate Vegas headpiece.

The scent of popcorn filled the air, and I saw that she'd been in the middle of making popcorn garland. "What are you talking about?" she asked, clicking the TV to "mute." She'd been watching *How the Grinch Stole Christmas*—the Jim Carrey version.

"You," I said. "Maybe doing a little nocturnal sneaking around. With Snoopy? And Woodstock."

Her brown eyes widened. She had her dark hair pulled up in a sloppy bun and wore a pair of plaid lounge pants and a *The* Ohio State sweatshirt. If her clients could only see her now—they might go back to a life of crime.

"You skipped the eggnog," she said, "and went straight for Kit's flask, didn't you? It makes sense, considering the dead Mrs. Claus and all."

Even though I hadn't known her well, there was an ache in my chest, a tug of grief for Lele. She had been a nice woman—at least toward me. Who had killed her? And why?

I plopped down next to Ana on the couch, and she offered popcorn from her bowl. "I'm perfectly sober."

"Then maybe I should get you a drink, because you're not making any sense. Snoopy?"

I eyed her. "Last night, someone set up a giant Christmas lawn decoration at my mother's house. One of those inflatable snow globe things—Snoopy and Woodstock. It's actually very cute."

Ana's mouth dropped open and a piece of popcorn fell out. She picked it off her lap and popped it back into her mouth, chewed, and swallowed. Suddenly, she started laughing. "An inflatable Snoopy snow globe? At Aunt Cel's?" She fell backward onto the couch cushions and kept laughing. Tears streamed from her eyes, and she held her stomach as if it ached. "Oh, oh! My stomach hurts. My cheeks, too. A snow globe. Priceless." She wiped tears away.

"You didn't put it there?" I asked, not sure I believed this fit of laughter wasn't to throw me off her scent.

"I wish I had. That's classic." She massaged her cheeks. "Oh, I wish I could have seen Aunt Cel's face this morning when she saw it. You don't know who did it?"

"I thought it was you!"

Ana shook her head. "Nope."

I crunched a piece of popcorn. "Then why were you late to my party last night? And don't tell me you were working. I'm not buying."

A guilty flush flooded her cheeks.

"Aha!" I accused.

"Aha yourself," she countered. "I wasn't at work, but I wasn't plotting the Great Snow Globe Escapade either. Though, really, I wish I'd thought of it."

"Then where were you?"

She rolled her eyes and set the bowl of popcorn on the table. "Trying to finish Kit's Christmas present," she said slowly.

"Finish his shopping?"

"No, his *present.*"

"You're making something?" She was the least crafty person, besides my sister Maria, that I knew.

She scrunched up her face. "No."

"I've had a long day and not a single drink," I said. "Could you just tell me? I don't have it in me for twenty questions."

"Promise not to laugh?"

I sat up, suddenly very interested. "Maybe."

She frowned at me, stood up, and pulled off her sweatshirt. "Whoa!" I said. "What're you doing? You're not taking one of those stripper pole gym classes to learn a few moves, are you? As a surprise for him?"

She winked at me. "Been there, done that."

"*Ew*! Too much information!"

She pulled up the back of her tank top. "See?"

I stared at the small of her back. "What am I looking at?"

"That." She twisted and pointed.

I leaned in, so close that my nose was almost touching her waistband. "Freckles?"

"Those aren't freckles."

"What are they?"

"It's the start of my tattoo."

Shocked, I looked up at her. "A tattoo?"

"Don't judge me."

"I'm not judging," I said, totally judging. Ana and a tattoo? Her mother would kill her. On second thought, Aunt Rosa had probably given Ana the idea. "I'm just a little surprised. Considering how you feel about needles." There were three or four little dots on her back. "Is it supposed to be a constellation or something?"

She sighed and pulled her shirt down. "It's supposed to be a heart with Kit's and my initials in it. But every time I go, and the needle touches my skin, I pass out. I've been there three times already. I tried again last night with the same result."

I pressed my lips together. Hard.

"You promised not to laugh!" she cried, tossing a piece of popcorn at my head.

"I said 'maybe,'" I mumbled.

"It's not funny, Nina."

My eyes watered, and I fanned them with my hand.

"What am I going to do? I can't think of a single other present for him."

The urge to laugh uncontrollably finally faded. "Yeah, considering you already did the stripper pole thing."

"Tell me about it. I should have saved that for Christmas. What was I thinking?"

I didn't want to know.

"Besides, I really wanted to do this for him," she said. "Show him I'm committed. Plus, you know how he likes tattoos."

"I think he likes you more." I wasn't sure about that at all—the man had the strangest fixation with ink. "He'll like anything you get him."

"You're not helping."

"Let me think on it."

"Think fast," she said. "Christmas is next Sunday."

"I will. So," I hedged. "Committed, eh?"

Ana wasn't known for long-term relationships.

Her cheeks colored. "I think so. Maybe. I don't know. I really like him, Nina. You won't tell him, will you?"

I smiled. I'd never seen her so head-over-heels. "My lips are sealed." I stood up. "I've got to go. I need to stop by Maria's on the way home. Apparently, she's acting strangely."

"More than usual?"

"She's baking."

Ana gasped.

"I know." As I pulled open the door, a big black blur barreled down on me. I braced myself as BeBe, Kit's massive mastiff, threw her paws on my chest and slobbered my face.

Kit followed behind her, carrying a bag of take-out Chinese food.

"Only action you'll see for a while with Bobby out of town," he said, winking.

I gave BeBe some love and attention, and said, "Don't remind me."

A few minutes later, I pulled into Maria's driveway. She lived in a McMansion on the edge of town. The house was done up much as my mother's—with dazzling white lights and tasteful decorations. I knocked on the door and waited. There was no noise coming from within at all—not even a yap from Maria's neurotic Chihuahua, Gracie.

As I climbed back into my truck, I could have sworn I saw a curtain shift in the upstairs window—one of the guest rooms.

I frowned and kept watching to see if it happened again. It didn't.

After a few minutes, I drove off.

It must have been only my imagination.

Chapter Six

Bright and early Monday morning, I sat in my office. I had a lot of paperwork to sort through and phone calls to return. 'Twas the season to set up garden makeovers for the spring.

I'd given everyone else the day off so I was a little surprised when I heard the front door of the office open.

"Hello?" I called out.

Brickhouse appeared in my doorway. Her hair was a bit perkier this morning, but her body hadn't returned to its normal brick-shape yet.

She clucked as she set a box of donuts on my desk, and I immediately forgave her for every insult she ever hurled my way. I picked through the offerings and said, "What're you doing here? You're not supposed to be back until tomorrow."

Leaning against the doorjamb, she shrugged. "Thought I would make sure you're not running this place into the ground."

I waved a glazed donut at her. "You're lucky you came bearing gifts, but suddenly I'm reminded of a certain Trojan horse."

Smiling, her eyes twinkled. She looked so much healthier than she had in the past few weeks. Her break from Mr. Cabrera was paying off.

Picking at the paint on door, she said, "The news isn't saying much about Lele McCorkle's murder. Is it true that Christmastowne is reopening today?"

Ah. The donuts had been in trade for information. Unfortunately for Brickhouse, I didn't know much. "It's true."

"The police are already done with their investigation?"

"No, but they've cleared the scene."

"Kevin hasn't told you anything?"

I shook my head. When he picked up Riley last night, he hadn't shared any information at all. Probably in retaliation for the video Kit made—which reminded me that I still needed to get that from him.

"And Fairlane?" Brickhouse asked. "She's not saying anything?"

I didn't mention that I'd seen Fairlane going into Mr. Cabrera's house last night. Some things Brickhouse just didn't need to know. "Not that I've heard. She's been keeping a low-profile since Saturday."

Since the murder.

Which was probably smart, considering that she may have been the intended victim.

When I mentioned that fact to Kevin, he'd grunted at me but didn't say anything. I hoped he took my theory seriously.

I set my donut down and frowned at it. Only the thought of a murder could make me lose my appetite for a Krispy Kreme.

Brickhouse said, "Do you still think it was supposed to have been Fairlane who was killed?"

"Everyone liked Lele. It doesn't make sense that she was the intended victim."

"What about her past?" Brickhouse asked.

"What about it?"

She clucked. "Maybe she has some skeletons in her closet?"

I poked at a flake of glaze clinging to my donut. "I don't really know anything about her past. Do you?"

"Not a thing."

Strange that we'd been neighbors for months, but I didn't really know much about the sisters. I didn't even know if either had been married. Or had kids or other family.

"*Ach.* I did hear that Lele wasn't happy at Christmastowne."

"You did?"

She nodded.

"Who said so? And why wasn't she happy?"

"Donatelli said Lele told him she didn't like working there. That she'd seen some strange things going on."

I put my hand up. "Wait, wait. First, *Donatelli* told you? When were you talking to Mr. Cabrera?"

She shrugged coyly. "He might have stopped by with some strudel yesterday."

"And you let him in?"

"I'm feeling much better these days."

Well, *Mr. Cabrera* wouldn't be if she found out about Fairlane's late-night visit to him. I rolled my eyes. "What kind of strange things?"

I wondered if it had anything to do with the missing toys Riley had noticed.

"Lele said she wouldn't share the 'sordid' details with him. That she wasn't a snitch."

"Sordid? That was her word?" Toy thefts might be called a lot of things, but sordid wasn't one of them.

Brickhouse nodded. "Makes you wonder."

It did. Sordid sounded like there might have been some hanky-panky going on behind all that tinsel at Christmastowne. But who had Lele been referring to?

More importantly, how could I find out?

The phone on my desk rang, and even though it was before office hours, I picked it up. "Taken by Surprise, Garden Designs, this is Nina."

"Nina, oh my God, you have to get over here."

It was a near-hysterical woman. "Who is this?"

"It's Jenny! Jenny Christmas."

Brickhouse had moved closer so she could eavesdrop, so I put the call on speakerphone. She'd brought donuts after all.

"Jenny? What's wrong?"

"Everything," she cried. "My whole life. But right this very minute? Every poinsettia you planted last week has shriveled up and died. I need you to get rid of the dead ones and replace them with new ones by the time the doors open at eleven."

I could feel my eyes widen.

Brickhouse clucked softly and shook her head.

"I'm not sure that's possible, Jenny," I said as gently as I could. There were hundreds of poinsettias at Christmastowne. Replacing them all would take a couple of days—not hours—and that was if my supplier had enough in stock. If.

"Make it possible, Nina," Jenny snapped. "I paid you a lot of money for those plants. Get me new ones, and get them now! Make it happen, or I will drag your name through the mud alongside mine. Got it?"

She hung up on me.

"Whoa," I said, staring at the phone.

"I never liked that Jenny Chester." Brickhouse clucked. "She made faces, too."

Obviously, Brickhouse could hold a grudge.

I stood up, then sat down, then stood up again. "We have to remove the dead plants at least. Can you call and see how many poinsettias our supplier has on hand?"

She nodded. "What do you think happened to those plants?"

I curled my hands into fists. One of them dying...I could see that. But *all* of them? There was only one answer. "Sabotage."

And whoever was behind it had just made it very personal.

Calling in help wasn't as easy as I expected, especially as today was a day off for my crew. Some of my employees either didn't have their phones turned on—or didn't answer them. So I did the only thing I could—promised lots of favors to friends.

"Thanks for helping me out," I said to the crowd gathered, trowels in hand. I glanced from face to face and felt a warm gush in my chest. These were the people I could count on when I needed them most.

"Anytime, Miz Quinn," Mr. Cabrera said.

My neighbors Flash Leonard and Mrs. Daasch nodded. As did Tam (with baby Niki strapped to her chest). I was beyond grateful anyone had responded to my SOS. "Kit will be here any minute with the replacement poinsettias, but for now, we need to start digging up the dead plants."

It had been a little over an hour since Jenny's call had come in, and we were gathered in Christmastowne's atrium. There were a hundred poinsettias—at least—in this area alone.

I fanned the pack out in pairs to tackle the uprooting, and I kept checking the door—not only for Kit, but because my parents had yet to show up. I thought they would have been here by now.

"Where you go, trouble always follows," a voice said behind me.

"You're not *always* trouble," I said as I turned. "Just most of the time."

"Ha ha. I wasn't talking about me," Kevin said.

"That's strange, because it feels like you're following me. First you're at my party, then you're an elf, now this. What's a girl to think?"

"Maybe I just can't stay away from you," he said, blinking his eyelashes.

A weird, warm fizzy feeling slid down my spine. I didn't like *that* one bit. Kevin and I were divorced. Done. That fizz was probably just a remnant of post traumatic stress from the breakup. "Now you're scaring me. Stop that."

He grinned a lopsided grin as if he could sense that fizz.

Damn him.

He nodded to the plants. "What happened?"

Safe ground. Thank goodness. "Looks like someone poured weed-killer over them." I picked up a shriveled plant. "Which had to take some time. Please tell me this place has security cameras."

"It does."

"Have you checked the film yet?"

"There's no film to check. Not from last night, when these plants bit the dust, and not from the day of Lele's murder."

"But you said..."

"Christmastowne has cameras, but they don't work. Someone tampered with the system on Saturday, and it's still not functioning."

I read between the lines of what he was saying. "Tampered with them before Lele's murder?"

He nodded.

I put two and two together. "Lele's murder was premeditated?"

"Sure looks that way."

I put the sad little poinsettia in a brown bag. "Do you know yet if she was the intended victim?"

"No proof otherwise." He plucked three plants from their bed and dropped them into the bag. He wiped his hands on his jeans.

I kind of missed his tights. Kevin had great legs. "Have you talked to Mr. Cabrera? He might have some information for you."

Great legs? I grabbed another plant and yanked. What was I even thinking about Kevin's legs for? I had Bobby now. *Bobby.*

Blond-haired, blue-eyed Bobby, who was the complete opposite of Kevin. Which was one of the reasons I liked him so much.

"Like what?" Kevin asked.

I told him what Brickhouse had said.

The lines around his eyes deepened as he said, "Sordid?"

I nodded. "And I've been thinking..."

"Dangerous."

I narrowed my eyes at him. "Do you know anything about Lele and Fairlane's backgrounds? Family? Where they lived before they came to the Mill? That kind of thing?"

"I'm looking into it, Nina. It's my case, remember?"

"Yeah, yeah."

He glanced around. "Did I see Mr. Cabrera around here with a trowel?"

"You did. He's working in the food court area, but you may want to stay away from Flash Leonard."

"Why?"

"He's not happy that his baseball disappeared after Lele was discovered. He thinks someone stole it and is going to try and sell it online."

"Was it signed?"

"I don't think so. He said he'd only get it autographed if there were old-timers here on Saturday—and there weren't."

"Then why does he think someone would sell the ball?"

"I think he puts a high price on sentimental value."

"Gotcha." Kevin's lips twitched. "I'll look into it. It's probably in the evidence room."

He looked up at the tree. "Did you know that someone cut the wires on the lights the day of the tree-lighting?"

"Really?"

"It's why the tree wouldn't light at first. Some quick-thinking elves spliced the wires together, but the tree will need to have the main cord replaced, sooner rather than later."

More sabotage. But why?

Over Kevin's shoulder, I spotted my parents coming in the front door. My mother was stomping like a pissed-off Nutcracker soldier, and my father trailed behind her, wearing his "patience" face.

Kevin turned to see what I was looking at and said quickly, "I'll talk to you later."

"Chicken," I called after him as he strode off in the opposite direction.

//

My mother's eyes were wild, bloodshot, and wide open in a crazy-person-on-the-loose kind of way. "We're here!" she cried.

I glanced at my father.

He said, "Thanks to me."

My mother just kept staring, wide-eyed.

"What's wrong with Mom?" I asked.

Dad smiled. Mom jabbed him in the chest. "This is not funny, Tonio. Not at all."

"A little," he said to me.

Mom let out a small cry.

"What happened?" I asked.

"We were backing out of the driveway to come here," he began.

"And it was on the roof," Mom said. "On. The. Roof."

I looked between the two of them. "What was?"

"A Santa Claus and nine reindeer. The Santa's arms move," she said, waving wildly.

I took it to be a mimic of Santa's abilities.

"Rudolph's nose blinks. Blinks like a freaking blinking beacon." She laughed a maniacal laugh.

"You can see it for miles," Dad said. "At least we don't have to worry about planes hitting the roof."

He might have himself a death wish, too.

"How long is this going to take?" Mom asked. "Because we have to take that Santa down. As soon as possible."

"I convinced your mother to come here first," Dad said.

"You owe me, Nina Colette Ceceri," my mother said, fisting my shirt and pulling me close. "You better have a good Christmas gift planned for me."

I, perhaps, needed to rethink the slippers and robe I was going to get her.

Because, even as we stood here, I could see snow starting to fall outside. Which meant that there was no way my father was getting on the roof to take down Santa today.

"How," I asked, "did someone put a Santa and reindeer on your roof without you noticing?"

"In addition to her ear plugs, she took one of her pills," my father said.

"What pills?" I didn't know she took any pills.

"A mild tranquilizer. It helps me sleep," Mom huffed, finally releasing me. "Don't judge me."

She'd been hanging out with Ana, apparently. There was a lot of non-judgment pleas going on these days.

I passed them both trowels and a brown lawn refuse bag. "Well, thanks for coming. Just dig up as many dead poinsettias as you can find."

"They look so sad," my mother said, glancing around. Then her gaze hardened. "But not as sad as that Santa on my roof after I get my hands on it." She stomped off, cursing loudly.

I looked at my dad. "Did you see the snow?"

He nodded.

"You might want to give her one of those pills now so she doesn't have a stroke."

He patted my cheek. "I've got it covered. She has about twenty minutes before she'll be down for the count. We'll keep this between us?"

I nodded.

"Good girl."

As he followed my mother's trail of curse words, I turned my attention back to work.

I'd dug up four plants before the fire alarm went off. Followed by the sprinkler system.

Chapter Seven

"At least the new plants are well-watered," Kit said an hour later.

I was still damp from head to toe. "Har. Har." My sense of humor had been drowned out of me. I looked like something washed ashore and just wanted to go home and crawl into a hot bath.

Kit had arrived after the fire department. The fire hadn't been in Glory Vonderberg's kitchen as I first assumed, but in a trash bin in the men's room.

Apparently, someone had dropped a lit cigarette into the trash and it had ignited crumpled paper towels. The fire had been contained, thankfully, and the sprinklers had only been on for a few minutes, but the damage had been done.

Christmastowne was a soggy mess.

"Chop, chop!" Jenny shouted from across the atrium as she clapped her hands loudly. "Get to work. We have one hour to get this place bone dry."

Kit looked at me. "Is she serious?"

"Delusional is more like it."

I didn't know how Jenny planned on explaining damp merchandise to her customers. Thankfully, the biggest draw, pictures with Santa, wasn't going to suffer. Santa's Cottage didn't have sprinklers inside it, so it had escaped the deluge.

"Uh-oh, she's headed this way," I mumbled, looking around for a place to hide.

"I'm out of here," Kit said.

"Don't leave me," I pleaded.

"You don't pay me enough to deal with that, Nina." He grabbed a pallet of poinsettias and trotted off.

I didn't pay myself enough to deal with it, either.

"Nina!" Jenny yelled as I turned to slink away.

Slowly, I pivoted and plastered a phony smile on my face. "Hi, Jenny."

"Look," she said, touching my arm, "I'm sorry if I snapped at you this morning. You cannot imagine the stress. And now the sprinklers?" She shook her head. "I feel like someone is out to get me."

And I felt like collateral damage. The sooner I wrapped things up at Christmastowne the better, but what she said resonated. It really did feel like someone was out to get her. "Do you have any enemies? Besides the thirty workers currently giving you dirty looks?"

She scowled. "They'll get over it."

I wasn't so sure. She was turning into a boss-from-hell.

"And no, I don't have any enemies. That's ridiculous. I was only kidding about someone out to get me. Why?" she eyed me. "Do you think someone's out to get me?"

Totally. "It just seems a little coincidental, all these things going wrong."

She chewed on her lip. Little bits of pink lipstick stuck to her teeth. "It does, doesn't it?"

"Is there any chance the fire this morning was set on purpose?"

Her brow crinkled. "I don't think so. The fire chief would have said so, right?"

I shoved another three dead—and now soggy— poinsettias into the bag. "Probably. Has anyone admitted to dropping the cigarette?"

"Not yet." She glared at her scurrying employees. "Coward."

Whoever it was probably feared for not only his job but his life. There was a dazed, crazed look in Jenny's bloodshot eyes that left me suspecting she was, in fact, capable of murder.

But I still doubted she had anything to do with Lele's death. It didn't make sense, unless I was missing something big.

I noticed that every hair on her head was fluffed and perfect. "How come you're not wet?"

Anger tightened her lips. "Because I was in Santa's Cottage when the sprinklers went off, firing Santa."

"What? You fired Drunk Dave?"

"He was drinking on the job again. Never hire family, Nina. I'm never going to hear the end of this at family gatherings." She shook her head, then looked at me slyly. "Speaking of hiring, I poached one of your hired hands to take over Santa's job. I hope you don't mind, but I was desperate to fill the position, and when I walked out of Santa's Cottage, there was the perfect man standing there. I asked, and he accepted."

I hoped she wasn't talking about Kevin. He couldn't pull off the elf look, much less a respectable Santa.

"Who?" I wavered between admiring her go-get-'em attitude and being really angry she hadn't asked me about it first.

"Donatelli Cabrera? He's starting as Santa this afternoon."

Mr. Cabrera? As Santa? I tried not to laugh. He wasn't a little-kid kind of person, though he tolerated teenagers fairly well.

"Good luck with that." Across the atrium, someone fired up a wet vac. "Are you sure opening today is a good idea?"

Her gaze snapped to me. "Yes. Today. No more delays." Her eyes filled with tears. "If this place doesn't turn a profit over the next few weeks, it's doomed, Nina. Then what will Benny and I do?"

I didn't have an answer for her, but seeing those tears helped me forget that I was miserable and wet and just wanted to go home. I would stay and help as long as she needed me.

It was, after all, what friends were for.

***

I was thinking about sabotage as I hauled a trash bag out to the Dumpsters behind Christmastowne.

It was a lot to think about.

Between the lengthy delays opening the village, the power outages, the wires on the Christmas lights having been cut, the fire in the men's room...

But if it was sabotage, who was the saboteur? And why? What was there to gain, other than to bring misfortune to Jenny and Benny?

Did they have any enemies? With the way Jenny snapped at her employees, I had a feeling any number of them might want petty retaliation against her. But enough to cause this level of destruction?

I propped open a fire door and sucked in a breath as a cold wind crawled under my skin. Snow fell in light flakes, dusting the back parking lot in a covering of white.

How did the missing toy donations factor into all this? In the midst of what had happened with Lele, I'd almost forgotten about the thefts. Was their disappearance part of the sabotage? If Riley was certain some were missing, I believed him. Little escaped that boy.

Then there was Lele. How did her murder factor in? Had it been a case of mistaken identity? Or had she seen the saboteur at work and was killed to keep her silent? Or did it have something to do with the "sordid" goings on she mentioned to Mr. Cabrera?

Snowflakes tickled my cheeks as I dragged the bag down a path to the Dumpster. All these questions were giving me a headache. For a second, I stopped, and just listened to the silence—that eerie, beautiful quiet of falling snow.

Then I came to my senses and realized I was freezing. I quickly finished dragging the trash to the Dumpster and heaved it over the side. On the way back, I saw that my footprints had already been covered up with snow. At the rate it was falling, Jenny wouldn't have to worry about opening on time—because no one would be going out in this weather.

I needed to herd my ragtag crew together and send them home before roads became too treacherous to travel. Picking up my pace, I frowned when I saw the door I left ajar firmly closed. I tugged on the handle, but it didn't budge. The makeshift door stopper I'd used had been dislodged by the wind.

Wonderful.

I banged on the metal door for a few minutes, the sound jarring in the snowy silence.

No one answered.

I glanced around. It was a long, frigid walk around the building. I grabbed for my cell phone and groaned when I saw it wasn't working. The screen had scrambled, and I realized it must have been damaged when the sprinklers went off.

As I stomped off, I realized how much I must have looked like my mother had this morning. It actually made me smile, which was a good thing, because I had a feeling that for a second there I had also shared my mother's going-to-kill-someone mentality.

Kicking into a jog, I silently thanked Duke, my trainer (who would love this story when I told him). His ceaseless treadmill training had finally come in handy. I jogged around the building and noticed a car parked at the edge of the lot, closest to me. The back windows were open, and the front ones were steamed.

What on earth?

As I drew closer, I heard a giggle, and the front windows powered down.

A flushed Santa, complete with beard and hat, said, "Ho ho ho!" when he saw me. "Who have we got here?"

A head popped up beside his and peered out.

Ho, ho, ho, indeed.

"Nina!" Fairlane exclaimed. "What are you doing out there? You'll catch a death!"

I cringed at the phrase, but it didn't seem to faze Fairlane. In fact, she didn't seem the least bit bothered that she was completely naked, either.

Santa, aka Drunk Dave, too.

I was going to need a therapist after all this.

"Locked out of the back door." I couldn't help but add, "What are you doing out here?"

As if it wasn't fairly obvious, with the nakedness and steamed windows. I just wanted to hear what she had to say for herself. I certainly wasn't looking at a grieving sister.

"Baby, it's cold outside," Santa said, slurring his words.

Fairlane giggled and said, "Santa, here, is just helping me celebrate!" She placed her hands on Dave's shoulders, and I noticed her fingernails had been painted a flaming red color. "I was rehired this morning."

This had to be Benny's doing. "Does Jenny know?"

//

"She doesn't call the shots around this place," Fairlane said, an arch to her eyebrow.

Santa made kissy noises at Fairlane. "Maybe you can put in a good word for me with Ben. Get me my job back. My wife ain't gonna be happy that I got fired."

"I'll try, Santa, baby," she cooed.

I thought I might be sick. I wiped snowflakes from my eyelashes. My rising temper counterbalanced the cold air. "I doubt your wife would be happy about *this*." I gestured to the car, the steamed windows, the *nakedness. Ick.*

"Ooh," Santa said. "The little lady wouldn't be happy. Oh no, sirree. That one has a temper, let me tell you. Best we keep this to ourselves," he said, winking.

Fairlane snuggled against him. "Nina's a party pooper, isn't she, Santa?"

I groaned and stomped away.

Fairlane called after me. "You'll keep this to yourself, right, Nina? Right?"

I pretended I didn't hear. It was a vastly better option that flipping her the bird, which was my first inclination.

As I pulled open the door to Christmastowne, I threw a look back at their car. It was rocking.

I was suddenly queasy and regretting that Krispy Kreme I ate this morning.

But I also wondered what Drunk Dave's wife would do *if* she found out that Fairlane had been boinking Santa?

Would she be mad enough to murder the faux Mrs. Claus?

Chapter Eight

"You're looking a little green around the gills, Abominable," Kevin said as I dripped melting snow all over Santa's Cottage.

Once back inside Christmastowne, I'd thanked my crew, told them I owed them all, and sent them home before they were all stranded here. Then I tracked Kevin to Santa's Cottage, eager to tell him about what I'd seen in the parking lot.

I borrowed a table cloth to dry off. "The things I've seen..."

Kevin sat in Santa's chair, taking notes in a tiny steno notebook. I knew he didn't need the information down on paper—his memory was impeccable, but he said writing things down helped him think more clearly. There was a furrow between his brows and as he looked at me, I saw troubled eyes.

"What's wrong?" I asked.

"More toys are missing."

"But the building's been closed—there haven't been any donations in days."

A corner of his lip quirked. "I set a little trap in Santa's chest. Someone bit."

"Who?"

There was an electric fire going in the faux fireplace. It emitted little heat, but enough that I wanted to climb onto the hearth and toast my tuchus. Nancy Davidson's camera bag and equipment was set up, ready to snap shots with Santa, but I didn't see her around.

"I don't know. Yet." He stretched a long leg. Pointing above the door, he said, "See that exit sign?"

"Am I blind?"

He rolled his eyes. "It's a hidden video camera, one that senses motion. Nancy Davidson helped me rig it up yesterday." He held up a tiny camera card. "As soon as I get home and load this onto my computer, our thief will be revealed."

Relieved, I sagged a bit. Riley was at school—he would be completely in the clear. But I also realized that whoever the thief was must work at Christmastowne. "How do you know the thief isn't Nancy?"

Kevin said, "I took a risk in asking for her help, but I figured if she was the thief she'd be smart enough to know she would be on camera if she stole the toys."

Nancy didn't seem like a thief to me. She seemed more like the Neighborhood Watch leader, with her keen eyes and seemingly boundless energy. "True enough."

Kevin raised one eyebrow and added casually, "You should get out of those soaked clothes right away, before you catch a cold."

I shivered, too cold to care about his not-so-subtle innuendo. "Gee, I forgot my change of clothes when I came to work to dig up some dead poinsettias and first got rained on by a sprinkler system, then when I was locked out in a blizzard."

"What's this about getting locked out?" He tucked his pencil into the spirals of the notepad and slipped it into his coat pocket.

"I went out back to the Dumpster and left the door propped behind me. The wind blew it shut."

His lip twitched.

"You better not laugh at me," I warned.

"Or what?"

I shoved a dripping lock of hair off my forehead. "Or you're going to see one seriously ticked-off Ninacicle."

He stood and crossed over to me in two long strides. He pushed my nose with his index finger. "No one wants to see that, but really, you need to get out of those clothes. You can borrow my elf costume."

"I'd rather have pneumonia." I cozied my backside up to the electric flames.

He shrugged out of his blazer and draped it over my shoulders. His shoulder holster fit snug against his white button-down, outlining his muscles. "Don't blame you. Those tights are enough to make a grown man cry."

"Now you know how women feel about nylons." I huddled into the warmth of the fabric and tried to ignore how his scent suddenly enveloped me. "As I traipsed around the building to get back inside, you'll never believe who I came across in the front parking lot."

"At this point, I wouldn't be surprised if Rudolph was out there."

"No, he's on my mother's roof."

"Do I want to know?"

"Probably. It's good for a laugh, but maybe another time. I saw Santa."

"Drunk Dave?"

"The very same. And he wasn't alone. He was with Fairlane."

"McCorkle?"

As if there was another. "She doesn't seem all that broken up by her sister's death, does she?"

"What makes you say so?"

"She was naked and playing with Santa's jingle bells." I explained about the steamed-up car.

He went to sit back down in Santa's chair, gave it a second look, and remained standing. "Just so you know, you're ruining Christmas for me."

"What I want to know is what might have happened if Drunk Dave's wife found out he couldn't keep his hands to himself. This probably wasn't the first time he and Fairlane hooked up."

Kevin smirked. "I'm not sure it's Dave's *hands* his wife has to worry about."

Truer words might never have been spoken. As Brickhouse had so eloquently put it, Fairlane was a hussy.

"Either way," I said, "Dave's wife might have a desire to see Fairlane dead—and may have accidentally killed the wrong sister."

Before I left Christmastowne, I went in search of Jenny. I passed through the empty reception area of the third floor office space—Jenny hadn't hired an assistant yet—and I found her sitting behind her desk, staring at a forty inch plasma TV. The local weatherman was predicting snowmaggedon.

I thought that a big dramatic of him. It was a snow storm, not the white death.

As I sat down, I noticed tears in Jenny's eyes. Outside the tinted windows, heavy snow fell. I couldn't even see my truck in the parking lot, which meant it was going to be a fun ride home. *Not.*

"I'm going to have to stay closed today," she said.

A ticker at the bottom of the TV screen listed all the local closings, including Riley's school. I wondered how he would get back to Kevin's and tried not to worry.

"It's probably best." It would certainly allow the place time to dry out. I glanced around. The divided office was spacious but sparse. Jenny's desk was neat as could be, without a stray paperclip to be seen. "The forecast calls for a warm-up tomorrow. All this snow will be gone by the weekend."

Letting out a deep breath, she leaned back in her chair. "I kind of wish the fire this morning burned this whole place down."

She seemed perfectly serious. "Really?"

"It's been nothing but a nightmare." She rubbed her temples.

Benny's desk was a mess, heaped with papers and files, old coffee cups and take-out containers. His side of the office was filled with pictures of himself in his old uniform, getting awards, and at media events. There were no other people in the shots. Only Benny.

Jenny's side only had one picture. Her wedding photo. She and Benny stood side by side, dressed in their finery. Jenny gazed adoringly up at Benny, while he gazed adoringly at the camera.

"Benny's not exactly camera-shy, is he?" I asked, standing to look at his pictures.

She smiled weakly. "There's no one he likes looking at more."

"Even you?"

"Even me, Nina." She sighed. "Now, what brings you up to my dungeon?"

Snowflakes flecked the windows. "All the dead poinsettias have been removed, but only half have been replanted. My crew will be back tomorrow to finish the job."

She narrowed her eyes on her watch. "Surely there's enough time to finish planting today."

"I sent my crew home already. The roads are getting dangerous."

Angry eyes flashed at me. "Unacceptable."

I stood up. I'd had enough of her abuse. "Technically, I don't have to be here at all, Jenny. The deaths of those plants don't fall under my warranty. Someone killed them on purpose. So I suggest you start taking a good look at your employees and try to figure out who's sabotaging this place. Because someone is. I'll see you tomorrow."

She said nothing as I left, and as I walked out, I nearly bumped into Benny.

By the guilty blush licking at his cheeks, it was clear he'd been eavesdropping.

Chapter Nine

The roads were a disaster. Cars in ditches, crawling traffic, and low visibility. I'd white-knuckled my steering wheel the whole way home. Not even the Christmas carols on the radio—or my new reindeer antlers—could relieve my anxiety.

I was never so glad to pull into my driveway in all my life, but was a little surprised to see ruts of tire tracks in the snow. Someone had been here recently.

Candy cane pathway lights led up to my front porch, which had been decked out as gaudily as possible with multiple strings of lights, dangling snowflakes, and icicles. Several light-up snowmen and painted ornaments were staked in my front yard. My mother's pawned-off snow globe was in my side yard but not currently inflated. It was a Christmas wonderland, and I loved it.

Bracing myself for the cold, I shouldered open the truck door and trudged through the blowing snow and ankle-high drifts. I skirted the house to go in the side door and noticed that the Snoopy snow globe would have to be dug out if I wanted to use it tonight.

I pushed open the door leading into the mud-slash-laundry room, and immediately a *yip*ping, *yap*ping ruckus started.

A tiny black ratlike creature barreled toward me, skidded on the linoleum, and knocked into my legs. As it continued its noisy welcome, I kicked off my boots and shrugged out of my coat. Bending over, I picked up the black blob. "Hi, Gracie."

My sister Maria's Chihuahua snarled at me. We had a history, Gracie and I. A *War of the Roses* (movie version) kind of history.

I petted her head, and she piddled on my arm.

Ah, hell. What was one more kind of wetness today?

I set her down, held my arm out to the side, and looked around. Where there was Gracie, there was usually Maria. "Hello?" I called out as I entered the empty kitchen.

"In here!" Riley shouted from the living room.

As I walked under the arch into the living room, I nearly had myself a heart attack at the sight before me.

"Don't you dare say a word," Riley warned.

I burst out laughing. "You're kidding, right? I'm on *Candid Camera*." I glanced around for any kind of hidden camera—including one lurking in an innocuous exit sign.

"Be nice, Nina," Maria chided. To Riley, she said, "Watch, Ry. Knit, knit, purl." Metal knitting needles clicked happily together.

The two of them sat side by side on the sofa, knitting.

Knitting!

Well, Maria was knitting. Riley was holding the ball of yarn. A big carpetbag sat on the floor. It was filled with dozens of skeins of varying colors.

Riley glanced up at me with big "help me" eyes.

"What are you both doing here?" I asked.

Riley said, "The street to Dad's was blocked off because of a big accident, so a buddy dropped me off here. Dad said he'd pick me up later."

"And you?" I asked Maria.

She primly set her knitting down. "I came by to drop off a few things. Look, I made you a scarf!" Rummaging in her Mary Poppins' bag, she came up with a folded purple scarf.

But as she reached out to give it to me, she suddenly pulled it back. "Why are you holding your arm out like that? And why is it wet?"

Riley sniffed. "Is that dog pee I smell?"

They gaped at me.

"Hey," I said, "it was Gracie's fault."

We all looked down at her, this half-deaf and mostly-blind dog. She was sniffing around the Christmas tree and making chortling sounds as though she was about to hack up a hairball. Maria called those noises "normal" for a Chihuahua.

There was a reason I didn't have a dog of my own.

"Well," Maria said, "I made this scarf for you." She shook it out, and it unfurled like a roll of toilet paper on the loose. It kept going and going. The scarf had to be six feet long, and was full of quarter-sized holes—slipped stitches. "Isn't it beautiful? You always look so pretty in purple. Not that you wear much of it."

My sister looked a lot like a young Grace Kelly and often behaved like a spoiled socialite. Despite our (very many) differences, she was my baby sister, and I (obviously) had a high level of tolerance.

But as much as I wanted to crack a joke at the state of that pitiful scarf, I couldn't. The pride in her eyes had me saying, "It's very nice."

She beamed, a magnificent smile.

Riley jumped up and headed for the door. "I'm going to shovel the front walk."

Which was probably pointless with the way the snow was coming down, but I recognized the opportunity to escape when I saw it. "Put on a hat!" He wore no coat, no gloves, nothing. Just his hoodie.

He threw me a withering look. Riley and I also had a bit of a *War of the Roses* history, but God, I loved that kid. And though he would rather cut out his tongue than admit it, I knew he felt the same.

I held back a smile as he reluctantly pulled the hood of his sweatshirt up over his head. The front door slammed behind him.

"I also brought a scarf for Mr. Cabrera," Maria said, digging again into her bag.

I sat on the edge of the couch, still holding my arm straight out like some sort of pee-drenched deranged toy solider. "When did you start knitting? And baking? And grocery shopping?"

Shrugging, she said, "Just trying some new hobbies."

Only Maria would think of grocery shopping as a hobby. "No, really," I pressed.

"What? I can be domestic."

"Is Nate pressuring you? Trying to change you?" I was ready to kick his ass if that was the case, despite the fact that I adored my brother-in-law. It took a special man to handle Maria long-term.

"Nina, no. I just thought I'd try some new things."

I peered at her carefully. "Are your roots showing?"

Her hand flew to the crown of her head, and she blushed. "I haven't been to the stylist this week."

"What is going on, Maria? 'Fess up."

She picked up her knitting, calm as could be. "Nothing is going on. I'm just maturing."

Aha! Now I knew something was up. Maria never used words like "maturing." At least not in reference to herself. But I knew by the set of her delicate lips that she wasn't going to give me any more information. I was going to have to do some snooping, maybe talk to Nate.

Gracie snortled again, and I glanced at her in time to see her squat on my Christmas tree skirt. More piddle.

I looked at Maria, who only knit faster.

"I'm going to take a shower," I said. "While I'm up there, I suggest you throw that tree skirt it in the washer, Ms. Maturity."

She stuck her tongue out at me.

That was more like it.

Through the window, I saw Riley pushing a shovel around. It was then that I noticed Maria's car wasn't parked out front. I started to get a funny feeling in my stomach. "Where's your car?"

"At home. Nate didn't want me driving in this storm, so he dropped me off on a way to a meeting downtown. He's going to pick me up later."

I watched the snow fall in a steady sheet. "How much later?"

"Tonight."

I held in a groan and prayed that Nate had four-wheel drive in his Mercedes so Maria wouldn't be stranded here overnight.

Sure, I had an abundance of tolerance, but a girl could take only so much.

Upstairs, I took a gratuitously long hot shower, blow-dried my hair so I wouldn't freeze to death, and cuddled in the warmth of my bathrobe. I sat on the edge of my bed, picked up my home line and dialed Bobby's cell phone number. I thought I would have heard from him by now with an update on his mom. Her surgery had been early this morning.

I worried my lip as the phone rang and rang. I was about to hang up when I finally heard him say, "Nina? I'm here."

He sounded tired. So tired. "Is everything okay?" I asked.

In the background, I could hear hushed voices. He sighed. "Not really. Sorry I haven't called, but I was waiting for more news."

I pulled on a pair of fuzzy socks. "What happened?"

"My mom had a stroke during the operation. She's in ICU now. It doesn't look good, Nina."

A lump wedged in my throat. As much as my mother drove me crazy—and she did—I couldn't imagine losing her. Ever. "I'm so sorry."

"Me, too," he said quietly.

I mentally went over my work list for the next few days. Could I skip out? Of course I could. What was the point of being boss if I couldn't play hooky once in a while? Kit was more than capable of handling the jobsite at

Christmastowne, and Tam and Brickhouse were the best office managers around. "I can take the next flight out."

"Isn't it the storm of the century up there?"

Damn! The snow. I'd forgotten. "I can drive down. My truck has four-wheel drive. I can be there by tomorrow morning. I'll drive all night."

"Nina." I heard a smile in his voice. "I don't want to have to worry about Mom *and* you. Stay put for now, okay?"

"But—"

"No buts. All you'll be doing down here is sitting around, watching the news, drinking stale coffee, getting groped by Mac."

"I could do without that last one," —been there, done that— "but those other things...I'd be doing all that with you. Holding your hand. Shoulder to lean on. You know, all that sappy stuff."

I looked at my bare ring finger. Bobby hadn't yet gotten around to buying me a ring for our engagement. I had a sneaky feeling he was waiting for the romantic Christmas trip we had planned at a little country inn.

There was a long pause before he said, "Stay put. I'll call when I have more news."

I didn't like that pause. "Bobby?"

"Yeah?"

I plucked at a piece of fuzz on my robe. "Nothing." I'd been about to ask if he'd make it back in time for our trip, but it seemed so trivial, so inconsequential, in the face of what he—and his mom—were going through. "I'll talk to you soon."

We hung up, and as I dressed in sweatpants and a long-sleeved tee, I realized I still had a lump in my throat.

But this one had nothing to do with Bobby's mother.

And everything to do with feeling like our relationship was about to undergo a drastic change.

Chapter Ten

I needed chocolate.

Gracie started barking as soon as my feet hit the stairs. I looked at her, waiting for me at the bottom of the steps, and said sternly, "Don't even think about peeing on my floor."

She must have sensed my mood and stopped yapping immediately. Looking up at me with her blank black eyes, her ears flickered. Then she turned and sniffed her way into the kitchen. I followed her and found Riley sitting at the kitchen island, chewing on a handful of mini marshmallows. His nose was red, his cheeks chafed.

"You dressed up for us, I see," Maria said as she set mugs on the counter.

She returned more and more to her normal self with each passing minute. I borrowed a phrase I'd heard a lot lately. "Don't judge me."

I motioned for Riley to give me his soaked hoodie as a smile played at the corners of Maria's mouth. I've always amused *and* irritated her. It was a package deal.

Riley didn't argue as he pulled the garment over his head. Thankfully, he had a T-shirt on underneath.

The washing machine was running as I stepped into the laundry room and threw Riley's sweatshirt into the dryer and set it for twenty minutes. I peeked out the side door and saw that the walkway Riley had just shoveled was already covered in two inches of snow.

Snowmaggedon didn't seem so dramatic anymore.

I clung to the hope that the meteorologists were right, and that the sun would come out tomorrow and melt all this white stuff away.

A girl could dream.

Back in the kitchen, Maria had her arms braced on the counter as she stared disdainfully at the container of Swiss Miss. "Please tell me that you have something other than packaged hot chocolate. Where's the good stuff?"

"That is the good stuff." Swiss Miss was my favorite.

She pouted. "You're kidding."

A nap sounded like a good idea right about now. "You could always go home and make your own fancy kind. Oh, wait, that's right. You're at my house. Uninvited."

"Snappy," Maria accused.

I sighed.

She pouted.

Riley bee-lined for the fridge, rooted around, and came out with a package of cookie dough. He handed it to me.

Did I mention how much I loved that kid?

Maria lifted one perfectly-plucked eyebrow. "Raw cookie dough? Don't you know how bad that is for you? Never mind the calories. The *fat*. The fat on your thighs. Even worse, your *hips*. What have your hips ever done to you, Nina?"

"Bite me."

She harrumphed and set the kettle on to boil. "Snappy," she murmured.

I slid a gaze to Riley. "Hold me back."

Sticking his hand into the marshmallow bag, he smiled and shook his head. "I missed it the last time you two got into it."

He was referring to a knock-down drag-out mud fight Maria and I had in her backyard a few months ago. Trust me, right now she should be glad that there was no mud around.

"I won that fight," Maria boasted.

I rolled my eyes and broke off a hunk of the cookie dough. I was trying my best not to worry about Bobby...and his tone. It was stress, was all. Nothing more. *Nothing more.* Perhaps if I kept telling myself that, I would believe it soon.

Riley said, "I wish I had a sibling to fight with. When are you going to have a baby, Nina?"

A chocolate chip wedged in the back of my throat. I grabbed my chest as I coughed, choking. Riley slapped my back. Maria ran around the counter, pushed Riley aside and wrapped her arms around me. She fisted her hands over my diaphragm and was just about to thrust when I gasped, "I'm okay." The chip had worked itself loose.

She thrust anyway.

"*Uhhhn!*" I cried, losing air.

"Is she breathing?" Maria asked Riley.

"She won't be if you keep doing that."

I elbowed her aside and sucked in a lungful of air. "Jeez, Maria!"

"Oh, that's the thanks I get for saving your life." She pouted.

"Next time let me die," I said.

"I will!"

I filled a glass of water and chugged it down.

Maria eyed me. "I told you that cookie dough was bad for you."

Lord help me. She was close to being kicked out in the storm. Only the thought of my mother's chastisement stopped me from booting Maria out.

The tea kettle was starting to whistle when I heard two raps on the side door before it squeaked open. "Ho, ho, ho!"

Gracie started yapping and as soon as Mr. Cabrera popped his head into the kitchen, she peed on the floor.

I shook my head. How much did that dog drink, anyway?

Mr. Cabrera looked from face to face, then said, "Bad time?"

"Nina's in a mood." Maria poured steaming water into the mugs.

I ate more cookie dough.

"That stuff ain't good for you, Miz Quinn," he said, pulling up a stool. "Think of the salmonella."

There was going to be bloodshed at my house tonight, I was sure of it.

"What're you doing here?" I asked, gripping my roll of cookie dough as though I might start swinging it like a bat. "Aren't you supposed to be working?"

"Working?" Riley asked, taking care of the newest puddle.

"Meet the new Santa at Christmastowne," I said, still amused at the thought.

"Ho, ho, ho!" Mr. Cabrera bellowed, shaking the windows.

Maria winced as she grabbed a mug for Mr. Cabrera. "You might want to tone that down a smidge. The kids might get scared."

His wrinkles deepened as he frowned. "Really?"

We nodded.

"You scared?" he asked Riley.

"A little," he said.

"It needs to sound merrier," Maria said, coaching him. "Like you're a jolly old fellow, not the scary Wizard of Oz."

Riley smirked. "Dude. Santa?"

Mr. Cabrera nodded. "Starting tomorrow. Jenny Christmas closed the place down today due to the weather. The best news is Fairlane McCorkle was hired back as Mrs. Claus, so maybe I can talk her into a date after all."

Ah. The real reason Mr. Cabrera took the job. "She does have a thing for Santas," I said, stuffing more cookie dough into my mouth and storing it in my cheeks like a little hamster.

"Your hips, Nina, your hips." Maria *tsk*ed.

There wasn't much of the cookie dough left to use as a weapon. Besides, I didn't want to waste it on her. "It's a long walk home, Maria."

Mr. Cabrera didn't like discontented females, so it was no surprise when he said, "I should get going. I was wondering if I could borrow the kid."

Riley jumped up. "I'm game."

"To do what?" I asked.

"Fairlane asked me to stop by," Mr. Cabrera said. "She needs some help getting a few things out of the storage space above her garage."

I imagined the conversation of her asking him to come over "some time" and he deemed that to be "right away." There was no lacking of optimism on his part.

Riley grabbed his sweatshirt from the dryer and pulled it over his head, *ahh*ing at the heat. I understood. There were some winter days I fantasized about crawling into the dryer myself. But my big hips and I would never fit.

"Wait! Before you go," Maria said. She ran into the living room and came back with her carpetbag. She pulled out a blue scarf and rolled it out.

It had to be eight feet long, and pockmarked just like mine.

"I made you a scarf, Mr. Cabrera!" she proclaimed.

His eyes widened and his mouth formed a wide *o*. "It's beautiful," he gasped, picking it up and wrapping it around his neck, four, five times. He separated the fabric so his mouth was clear and said, "Thank you, Miss Maria." He kissed both her cheeks.

My heart fluttered. That Mr. Cabrera was a good guy. You know, if you took away all the dead girlfriends and everything.

"Don't worry, Riley," Maria said. "I'm still working on yours."

Riley's eyes widened in terror. "You don't have t—"

Mr. Cabrera elbowed him.

"*Uhn.* I mean, thank you," Riley said.

I saw them off through the side door and came back into the kitchen to find Maria sneaking a chunk of cookie dough. "Aha!"

She blinked innocently. "I'm only thinking of your hips."

The phone started ringing, and I snatched up my cookie dough before she polished it off. Then I glanced at the Caller ID and picked up the phone. "Nina Quinn's halfway house."

Maria flipped me off.

I smiled.

"I just have to stop at home, then I'll be over," Kevin said. "And have I got news for you. You're not going to believe what was on that video tape."

Chapter Eleven

By the time Kevin knocked on the door ten minutes later, it looked like the snow was lightening up a little.

Or maybe that was wishful thinking on my part.

Gracie barked, peed.

Maria sighed and went for paper towels.

As soon as I pulled open the door, Kevin thrust a package at me. "This was jammed in your mailbox."

I took the manila bubble envelope from him, and my heart squeezed a little at the sight of Bobby's name on the return address. Then I frowned when I realized the address was in Texas, and that nagging lump in my throat was back.

Kevin stomped his way inside, wiping his boots on the mat by the door. Gracie took one look at him and went running. She bumped into the edge of the couch before diving under the coffee table.

Sometimes when I saw Kevin, I felt that way, too.

Maria came in carrying a roll of paper towels. "Pee patrol," she said at Kevin's quizzical glance.

"The rat?" Kevin asked, referring to Gracie.

"No, Mr. Cabrera," I teased. "You just missed him."

Kevin smiled and shrugged out of his jacket. He hung it on a hook by the door.

"You got here fast," I said, trying to resist the lure of Bobby's envelope.

"The entrance to my street is closed. The accident earlier knocked out power and broke a water main."

A steady pulse of panic threaded its way through my veins. "When's it supposed to open up again?"

He wouldn't look at me. "Tomorrow."

I groaned.

"You don't mind if Ry and I stay here tonight, do you?"

Was that a trace of humor in his voice? I glanced at him, at his sparkly green eyes. Damn it. It was. "I'm sure Mr. Cabrera will be happy to put you up. Ry can stay with me."

"Party pooper."

I grunted. That was twice today I'd been called that.

Kevin nodded to the envelope in my hand. "You gonna open that?"

"Later," I said, tucking it under my arm. The last thing I wanted was an audience. "What was on that video tape?" My curiosity was killing me.

"Do you have a laptop? I'd rather show you."

Nodding, I said, "I'll get it."

As I ran up the stairs, I heard Kevin ask Maria, "Are you staying over, too?"

"I think so," she said.

Ugh. There wasn't enough cookie dough in the world.

Even though I was dying to see what Bobby had sent, I wanted to see that tape more. I dropped his package on my bed and grabbed my laptop from my nightstand. Back downstairs, Kevin slipped in the tiny disk. "I watched this at the station. My unofficial investigation into those toy thefts just got very official. And this tape might just break open Lele's murder case as well."

The screen was dark at first, then came to life when someone stepped into Santa's Cottage.

"Where is that?" Maria asked, leaning over the back of the couch to see the screen.

I explained about Christmastowne.

"It's adorable!" she exclaimed.

It really was—if one didn't count the murder and all the strange things happening there.

The shadowy figure came into the light and looked around. I gasped.

It was Fairlane McCorkle.

She peeked out the door, took a quick look in the back room, and then quickly walked over to Santa's chest and scooped up the presents Kevin had put in there as bait. She opened her enormous handbag and dropped them in.

My jaw dropped. "That sneak!"

"Wait," Kevin said darkly. "It gets better."

Maria came around the couch and scooched in next to me. Which pushed me firmly up against Kevin. The heat of his leg blistered against my thigh.

I wiggled closer to Maria.

"Stop fidgeting," she demanded.

I elbowed her.

"Hey!" she cried.

"Do I need to separate you two?" Kevin asked.

I thought it might be better if he moved, but I kept my mouth shut.

"Why does she keep looking at her watch?" Maria asked.

"She's waiting for someone," Kevin said, a hint of laughter in his voice.

A minute passed where Fairlane strolled around Santa's Cottage, nicking ornaments and even a candy cane. She peeled that and started eating it.

Another minute passed and we watched as Fairlane's head snapped up. Someone had come into the cottage. The shadowy figure drew closer to her and took her into his arms. I squinted at the screen.

"Wait for it..." Kevin said.

The man spun her around and kissed her.

My jaw dropped as I looked at Kevin, at Maria, then back at the screen. I was speechless.

Finally, I said, "I think I'm gonna be sick."

"Who's the hottie?" Maria asked.

"Benny Christmas," I said.

"Benny Christmas," she echoed. "I spit on his name. *Pattoey!*" she mocked spit.

"How do you really feel about him?" Kevin asked.

"He killed Carrie Hodges. Do you remember her, Nina? She was so sweet."

"Technically," Kevin said, "he didn't kill her."

"He was drunk," Maria countered.

"Not quite, and she was the one who crossed the line," Kevin pointed out.

Maria fisted her hands. "Well, if he had been sober, he could have swerved to avoid her."

"Maybe," Kevin said. "Maybe not. It was an accident."

"I used to like you," Maria said, huffing.

"Wait, wait, wait!" I cried. "Back up, Maria. How do you know Carrie Hodges?" Because I certainly didn't know her.

"She was on my cheer squad in high school," Maria said. "She was a freshman when I was a senior. I was cheer captain, you know," she said to Kevin.

"I know," he said.

Everyone knew.

But that explained why I didn't know Carrie. I would have long been out of high school when she was there.

"Her funeral was the saddest thing I've ever seen. She was an only child, and her mother looked like she wanted to crawl into the grave right along with her daughter." She shuddered.

I shuddered, too. What a horrible loss.

I glanced at Kevin. Once upon a time, we'd talked about having kids, but first I'd wanted to get my business up and running. Then our marriage fell apart.

Bobby and I had talked about kids, but now, with him gone, those discussions seemed a very long time ago.

On the video, Benny and Fairlane groped each other for a few minutes, before they seemed to get into a heated discussion.

"Is there no audio?" I asked.

"No," Kevin said. "But I assume this is the part where Fairlane asks for her job back."

"Actually," Maria said, "she's threatening him that if he doesn't give her job back, she's going to tell his wife about their affair."

Kevin and I stared at Maria.

"What?" she said. "I can read lips."

"Since when?" I asked.

"Since college. I took a course on it as part of learning how to do sign language."

"You know sign language?" I asked.

She glared at me. "Yes, Nina. Jeez, don't you know me at all?"

I was beginning to think the answer to that was no.

Kevin said, "You'll want to see this next part."

"There's more?" I asked.

"Oh yeah."

The tape continued on, showing Benny giving in to Fairlane's demand. She groped him some more, then left. As soon as she did, he sat in Santa's chair, and dropped his head into his hand.

"Scum," Maria muttered.

We ignored her. Benny sat there for a little bit before looking up at the doorway. He smiled as a woman came inside, hiked her skirt up to her waist, climbed atop his lap and straddled him. She tossed her hair, and I got a good look at her profile.

It was Glory Vonderberg.

"Is that his wife?" Maria asked.

"Nope," Kevin said.

"He does like himself a cougar, doesn't he?" Maria said.

Apparently.

Glory reached for Benny's belt and started unbuckling. Benny unbuttoned her shirt, revealing a lacy red bra.

"At least she has good taste in lingerie," Maria said.

I was thinking this tape was about to get very X-rated when suddenly both Benny and Glory froze. Benny said something.

Kevin and I looked at Maria.

She translated. "He said, 'Did you hear that?'"

On the tape, Glory nodded. Her lips moved but with the angle of the camera, it wasn't clear what she said.

They paused for a moment, then started with their unbuttoning and unbuckling again. There was much kissing going on, and I could only imagine the slurping and suckling noises.

Suddenly, they froze again, and looked toward the back room of the cottage. Benny's lips moved.

"He said, 'Is anyone back there?'" Maria looked at us. "As if someone would answer."

She had a point.

Benny and Glory quickly resumed their exploration of each other. Just as Glory unzipped Benny's pants, they jumped apart.

Maria leaned in. "Benny cursed, then said something about a fire alarm?"

"The fire alarm went off this morning at Christmastowne," I said. "Complete with sprinklers."

"That explains the woman freaking out about everything getting wet," Maria said.

The pair on the screen waited near the doorway, then Benny patted Glory's rear and they went out the door.

//

But not before a shadow appeared in the doorway behind them—the one leading to the back room of the cottage.

The tape went black.

"Did you see that?" I asked.

"What?" Kevin went to take the disk out of the computer, and I slapped his hand.

"Go back to the last shot."

Maria said, "I don't think I can watch the two of them fondle each other again. I have a sensitive stomach."

"Not that part," I said. "Just the very end."

Kevin scrolled through video.

"There!" I cried. "See it?"

Sure enough, there was someone in that doorway. Someone who had been in Santa's Cottage the whole time?

"Do you know who it is?" Maria asked.

"Hard to tell," Kevin said.

I let out a breath. "I know who it is."

"Who?" Kevin asked.

"It's Jenny Christmas."

"How do you know?" Maria asked. "The tape isn't very clear."

My stomach turned at the thought of what Jenny must have seen. I looked between Maria and Kevin, and said, "Because she told me."

Chapter Twelve

I explained to them how Jenny told me she'd been in Santa's Cottage when the sprinklers went off—firing Santa, aka Drunk Dave.

"She obviously lied about the timeline," Maria said.

The lights on my Christmas tree cast a colorful glow on the walls. A fire crackled in the fireplace, and the scent of vanilla hung in the air, thanks to a few lit candles. It was all so cozy, yet I felt a chill. A chill that seeped into my soul.

"Where do you stand in Lele's murder case?" I asked Kevin.

Kevin removed the disk from my computer. "I spent most of yesterday trying to get background on Lele. Unfortunately, Fairlane wasn't talking, and I didn't have much else to go on. I ran a simple background check on both of them, and I didn't find anything."

"Nothing?" Maria asked. "Not even a parking ticket?"

"*Nothing*," Kevin said. "Neither have a history. You know what that means, right?"

My eyes widened. "Aliases?"

He nodded. "I called over to the county coroner and asked him to take fingerprints from Lele and fax them to me."

Maria shuddered. "That's gross."

Again, I agreed with her. What was the world coming to?

"I ran the fingerprints through the system," Kevin said. "I just got the results. Turns out Lele was Leigh Ann Walters, and Fairlane is Elaine Walters. The two sisters have rap sheets three pages long. Theft, fraud, forgery, embezzlement, bribery, blackmail. They're con artists who specialize in going after rich men and taking them for all they're worth."

"Both of them?" I could see Fairlane...but Lele? Sweet, shy Lele?

"Apparently, Lele was the mastermind, while Fairlane did the dirty work," Kevin said.

Wow. I leaned back against the sofa cushions. Just wow. "So, they were at Christmastowne just to get their hands on Benny?"

Kevin nodded. "Seems so. The toy donation thefts were probably secondary. Too good to pass up."

"Why Benny?" I asked.

Kevin said, "They probably saw that documentary on him and heard about the huge settlement he won against Carrie Hodges's insurance company. He got millions."

Millions of which he sank into Christmastowne. But maybe the McCorkle sisters didn't know that.

"Well," Maria said, examining a fingernail, "we know that Fairlane blackmailed Benny to get her job back. Perhaps Lele blackmailed him, too, without her sister knowing? Looking for a big payout for herself? She had to have known Fairlane was sleeping with him."

It kind of made sense. "She had talked about sordid things going on at Christmastowne to Mr. Cabrera," I said. "Why would she have done that? It implicated her sister."

"Does Mr. Cabrera have money?" Kevin asked.

I nodded. "Not that he shows it."

Kevin lifted his brows. "She might have been targeting him, trying to get on his good side, playing with his sympathies."

"Playing with fire," I said. "She had to have heard about the curse."

"Maybe she didn't believe it."

"She's dead, isn't she?"

Kevin smiled. "Hey, you don't have to convince me. I've seen that curse firsthand."

Me, too. I shuddered.

Maria leaned forward. "Maybe Benny didn't want to pay Lele's price and killed her because of it! He totally looks like a killer."

Maria wasn't going to let this go. "A minute ago you called him a hottie," I said.

"I clearly lost my mind for a second there."

I could buy that. It happened a lot with Maria.

"He deserves to be in prison," she added.

I ignored her. Seemed to me that Benny had paid the price for drinking that night. He'd almost died, too, and had also lost a career.

Kevin said, "Blackmail is a strong motive. Benny wouldn't want Jenny to know about his affairs."

Kevin would have firsthand knowledge about that. Since he'd cheated on me...

Forgiveness, I told myself.

But dammit, forgiveness was hard. Even after he'd almost paid the price for his indiscretion with his life. Thankfully, for Riley's sake, the bullet Kevin had been hit with hadn't been fatal.

Okay, and for my sake, too.

As mad as I had been at him, I didn't want to see him dead.

Maimed a little, but not dead.

"Whether it was Fairlane or Lele, or both, who were blackmailing him," Kevin said, "the question remains if this murder is a case of mistaken identity."

Aha! He had been listening to me, after all.

Kevin went on. "Fairlane, whether she realized it or not, was a big risk for Benny, especially after she blackmailed him to get her job back. He might have realized she was a loose cannon and thought killing her would be the best way to shut her up. He could have thought he was killing Fairlane Saturday morning, but killed Lele by mistake." He explained to Maria about how Fairlane had been fired and how Lele took her place as Mrs. Claus.

I added to this theory. "When I saw Benny before the tree-lighting, he was shocked to hear that Jenny fired Fairlane. He had no idea. So he could have easily thought Lele was Fairlane—especially if he snuck up behind her."

We sat in silence for a minute, letting it all sink in. Finally, I said, "But it seems like Jenny has motive, too. She's gung-ho on seeing Christmastowne thrive. If she knew Fairlane or Lele was blackmailing her husband, she might have killed to keep the news from leaking out. Part of Christmastowne's appeal is Benny's tie to it. It's his name, his career, his accident, his recovery that will bring people in. The All-American Hero, remember? Would they still come if they knew he was a serial adulterer? I don't think Jenny would want to take that risk."

And I knew right at that instant Jenny had probably known about Benny's affairs all along. She turned a blind eye to get what she wanted—a successful business. It made me realize that I hardly knew her at all.

Maria nodded. "I could see that."

Kevin leaned back on the cushions and rubbed his temples.

I said, "I still don't know how either of them would have been able to move the body, though, without anyone seeing."

Kevin said, "Many witnesses place Santa dragging a large, lumpy velvet sack around Christmastowne that morning, but no one can say for sure if it was Drunk Dave in the Santa costume. I've already sent the sack to the lab for testing. And," he added, "those enormous presents were placed under the tree just before Lele's body was discovered. It would have been simple enough for someone to put Lele under a box and wheel it to the tree. It wouldn't have aroused suspicion."

"Has anyone admitted to putting the exact box Lele was found beneath under the tree?"

"Several people unloaded boxes, but no one said they saw anything suspicious. I suspect that whoever put Lele under the box did so after the box was already under the tree."

I sighed, remembering the chaos of that morning. "I suppose we can't rule out that Fairlane may have killed her sister, too. Maybe she got sick of splitting their proceeds? Or of sharing the Mrs. Claus limelight. Remember how she wasn't too happy that people always seemed to like Lele and that she never got fired? Maybe there's a jealousy factor. Have you questioned Fairlane formally yet?"

Kevin said, "She lawyered up right away, probably figuring the truth of her identity would come out. I have an appointment to speak to her—and her lawyer—tomorrow at the station."

"At least Fairlane doesn't seem eager to leave town," Maria said, trying to lure Gracie out from under the table. The dog wasn't budging. "Not if she wanted her job back at Christmastowne and is having Mr. Cabrera and Ry take her Christmas things down from the garage attic."

Kevin looked around. "What? Ry's not upstairs?"

"He's helping Mr. Cabrera over at Fairlane's."

Kevin jumped up. "I don't think that's a good idea. She could be a killer."

My stomach sank.

"Way to go, Nina," Maria said, then yelped.

I might have "accidentally" kicked her. "I didn't know!"

"I'll go get him," Kevin said. "Maybe ask Fairlane some questions while I'm there."

"Officially or unofficially?" I asked.

"Officially unofficial."

I stood up, too. "Well, I'm coming along."

He looked about to argue, but gave a quick nod instead.

"Don't worry about me," Maria said. "I'll stay here, all alone. By myself."

"Oh, all right, you can come, too," I said as I put on my coat.

She jumped up with a *squee*. "Don't forget to wear your new scarf!"

Maria brought it to me, and wrapped it around my neck. And wrapped. And wrapped.

Kevin grinned evilly. "Did you make that yourself, Maria?"

She nodded. "Do you like it?"

He adjusted the fabric so it covered my mouth. "It's perfect for Nina. *Owl*"

I might have "accidentally" kicked him, too.

As we trooped outside, I saw that Riley had uncovered the snow globe and plugged it in. Inflated, its top was covered in snow, but Snoopy and Woodstock were aglow.

Maria wrinkled her nose. "Really, Nina?"

"It was a gift, but I love it."

"A gift from whom?"

"Mom."

Maria stumbled in the snow. Kevin grabbed her arm. "You're kidding," she said.

"Nope." As Kevin trudged ahead of us, I explained what was going on at our mother's house.

Maria, instead of finding it amusing like me, said, "That's disturbing. Who would do such a thing?"

Who, indeed?

I'd ruled out Ana. And Maria, too—her outrage was genuine. Who else knew my mother's eccentricities so well? Only someone close to her would understand how these pranks would get under her skin.

I wasn't sure who, but I had an idea how to find out, thanks to Nancy Davidson. I was going to get myself one of those motion cameras and hook it up at my parents' house... But when I discovered the identity of the prankster, I wasn't sure whether I should turn him in or buy him a drink.

Another snow burst was moving through, and by the time we reached Fairlane's garage, another inch had fallen. Inside the garage, we found Riley standing at the bottom of a ladder leading to an attic access in the ceiling.

There was only one box with "XMAS" marked on it at his feet. "Only one box?" I asked. "You've been over here almost an hour."

"Well," Riley said, dragging the word out. "First, we waited and waited for Fairlane, but if she's home, she's ignoring us. The garage was open, though, so Mr. Cabrera finally decided we should get started without her."

"I can't hear you, boy!" Mr. Cabrera said. He stuck his head into the attic opening. "Oh! You weren't talkin' to me. HO, HO, HO, hello!" he exclaimed.

"Better," Maria said, encouragingly.

He disappeared again.

Riley said, "Second, Mr. Cabrera lost his footing and almost fell through the rafters, but he insists he be the one to bring the boxes down. He's a stubborn old man."

Yes, yes he was.

Kevin said, "I'll go help him."

"So, Fairlane's not around?" I asked as Kevin headed up the ladder.

I might have admired his backside. Just a little. Sue me.

"She's probably visiting around the neighborhood," Riley said. "Her car's here."

It was parked in the driveway, covered in snow. I looked across the street, at Mrs. Greeble's empty house—she'd moved to a retirement home a few weeks ago and the house was now up for sale. My gaze skipped to Flash Leonard's home. Maybe Fairlane was there, trying to con him out of his life savings. I was going to have to warn everyone about her.

Maria snooped around the garage. She turned the handle on the door connected to the house and it swung open.

"What are you doing?" I asked.

"Looking for evidence," she said.

"Maria Ceceri Biederman, close that door right now."

"Evidence of what?" Riley held the ladder steady as his dad heaved himself into the attic.

"Long story," I said.

Above us, a cry rang out. Then a loud bone-jarring crash.

Kevin yelled out, "Call 911! Mr. Cabrera's fallen through the ceiling."

Riley whipped out his cell phone, while Kevin jumped through the attic opening, ignoring the ladder. He ran to the door to the house and whipped it open.

Maria said, "Oh, so it's okay for him to go in?"

I ignored her and followed Kevin inside. Riley and Maria followed me. The house was neat as a pin and sparsely furnished.

"Mr. Cabrera!" Kevin called.

"In here." The loud shout came from a room at the end of a long hallway.

Kevin turned the knob on the door, and we each bumped into each other as he stopped short.

My eyes widened as I took in the room—completely covered in piles and piles of toys and merchandise—undoubtedly all stolen. It was a shoplifter's paradise.

Mr. Cabrera said softly, "Please don't tell me she's dead."

Kevin rushed inside as I said, "Dead? Who's dead?"

"Stay back," Kevin warned us as he knelt next to Mr. Cabrera. "Don't move," he told him. "An ambulance is on its way."

"Dead?" Maria echoed, crowding the doorway, trying to see into the room. "Who's dead? Not Mr. Cabrera!"

"No," Riley said, pointing. "Her."

I gasped. Fairlane lay on the floor near the closet door. A pair of striped tights was wrapped tightly around her neck.

Unfortunately for Mr. Cabrera, she was most definitely dead.

Chapter Thirteen

A few hours later, I checked the clock and glanced out the window again. The porch light, lamppost, and various decorations illuminated the snow and little else. Still no sign of Kevin. I hadn't seen him since shortly after Fairlane's body had been discovered.

Mr. Cabrera had been taken to the hospital because of a cut on his head, and the doctors wanted to keep him overnight for observation in case he suffered a concussion. Otherwise, he was just fine, thank goodness. Last I heard, he had company. Brickhouse had fought her way through the storm to be by his side.

Snow continued to fall, and I was feeling a bit betrayed by the meteorologists. There was no way all this snow would be gone by the weekend. There had to be ten inches outside already. A veritable blizzard by Cincinnati standards. The city—and outlying areas—would be closed for days. Riley's high school had already called off classes for tomorrow, which was supposed to be his last day before Christmas break. He was going to be thrilled.

Currently, he was up in his room playing video games. Maria was in my room, tucked into my bed, snoring on my pillows. Once the clock struck nine, she couldn't stop yawning and turned in. Nate had been stranded downtown and had luckily scored a hotel room within walking distance of his office.

Soft Christmas carols played from overhead speakers as I put a pot of coffee on and took my package from Bobby into the living room. Gracie slept in front of the hearth and lifted a sleepy head when I came in, but didn't bark or piddle, so I figured my night was looking up.

Flames crackled in the fireplace as I sat on the sofa. I drew an afghan over my lap and stared at the envelope Bobby had sent. I had wanted a little privacy when opening it. A very young, girly part of me wanted a long sappy love letter. After all, it had been weeks since I had seen him, and we'd had startling little communication in that time. He was busy with his mom—I understood that—but I was beginning to feel like he'd forgotten about me.

I carefully tore the perforated strip along the top of the bubble envelope, took a deep breath and reached inside. A gurgle of anticipation grew in my stomach. My fingertips felt a bit of plastic inside the envelope, and I pulled.

And stared at what came out.

It was an Almond Joy. Or used to be, at least.

Somewhere along the package's journey, the Almond Joy had melted, pooling on one side of its wrapper, where it hardened once again. One side of the candy bar was a hard round blob, the other side flopped with emptiness.

I didn't know whether to laugh or cry.

The first present I ever got from Bobby was a case of Almond Joys, after I'd had a bit of a sugar-crash in his former office and he'd given me a candy bar to stave off a compete meltdown.

This candy bar, as misshapen as it was, was a reminder of how we'd began. It was his way of letting me know he was thinking of me. *Awww.*

I billowed the envelope and looked inside for a note, but there was nothing else inside the package. Tipping it upside down, I shook it, just in case I missed something obvious.

Nothing.

No note, no professions of love, no ooey gooey "I miss you."

Just the melted chocolate. Which no longer looked as endearing.

He was a writer, for goodness' sake. How hard could it be to come up with a few lovey-dovey lines? I put the candy bar back into the envelope and put it on the coffee table, not sure what to make of my feelings.

Wasn't absence supposed to make the heart grow fonder?

I was still thinking about that as I wandered back into the kitchen and poured a cup of coffee. After stirring in liberal amounts of cream and sugar, I sipped contentedly. I washed some dishes, put the tree skirt into the dryer, foraged for a snack (popcorn), and glanced out my kitchen window at Bobby's house across the street. Part of me wished he'd suddenly appear.

Kit's truck wasn't in the driveway, and I figured he was spending the night at Ana's—which was something of a regular occurrence lately. So much for house-sitting.

I munched on a piece of popcorn and told myself to stay strong. Support Bobby as best I could. That's what mattered right now—not stupid love notes.

My cell phone chirped an alert for a text message, and I almost didn't recognize the noise. Riley had placed the SIM card in my dead cell phone into my old cell phone. I was glad to have a working cell, but my old phone was practically vintage. It had an antenna and everything. I tore myself away from staring at Bobby's place and checked the text message. It was from Ana, and the subject line was "Ha ha ha!"

I could only imagine. I opened the file, a photo, and started laughing.

It was a shot of a snowy lit-up Santa and nine reindeer atop a house.

My mother's house.

I texted Ana.

Me: *Are you out in this storm?*

Her: *maybe*

Me: *Crazy.*

Her: *worth it 2 see Santa*

Me: *Don't let my mom see you.*

Her: *not stupid don't have death wish*

I didn't mention how stupid it was to venture out on a night like tonight to get a glimpse of my mother's Santa.

Smiling, I left the conversation at that and slipped my phone in my robe's pocket.

Peeking out the side door, I watched as crime scene techs stamped all over Fairlane's yard. Big lights had been set up, illuminating half the road, and police cars and tech vans lined the street. The coroner's vehicle had already come and gone.

I wanted desperately to forget about Fairlee and Fairlane. To forget that crime could happen so close to home. Forget that evil existed. Fairlane lived just a few houses away—and someone had broken in and killed her.

I shuddered, turned away from the window, and went to refill my coffee.

It was going to be a long night.

I heard footsteps on the stairs and a second later Riley came into the kitchen, looking more and more like his dad everyday. The mop of unruly hair, the shape of his eyes. "No sign of dad yet?"

"Not yet," I said, leaning against the sink.

He poured himself a cup of milk, then grabbed a package of Oreos. "It'll probably be a late night. You think Mr. Cabrera will be released soon?"

I shook my head. "He's spending the night at the hospital."

Riley's face scrunched. "Then where's Dad gonna sleep?"

Oh, jeez. I'd forgotten Kevin was going to spend the night at Mr. Cabrera's. For cryin' out loud. I sighed. "He can stay here." I had no idea *where*. Maria was in my bed—and I was not sharing with her—she kicked and thrashed when she slept. I was on the couch. Riley only had a twin bed...

Riley smirked—again, looking a lot like his dad. "You're a softie."

"Don't remind me."

He went back upstairs, taking the whole package of cookies with him, the little devil.

I tried watching a movie for a while, but couldn't get into it. Also tried reading, but after reading the same page three times and having no idea what it said, I put the book down. Instead, I gathered up my sketch book and supplies and nestled into the couch. I penciled in a garden, done all in shades of purples. Lavender, tulips, aster, sweet pea, irises, lupine, violets, monkey-flowers, vinca. I drew, I colored, I shaded. The artist in me was in heaven.

A little after midnight, I heard a tap on the backdoor. I set my things aside and went to let Kevin in. He kicked off his shoes and hung up his coat.

I felt a pang at the familiarity and pushed it aside.

He looked bone tired. "Coffee?" I asked. "Or will it keep you up all night?"

He smirked. "Too late for that."

I poured him a cup, and he settled in on the couch, staring at the flames leaping in the grate. Gracie, thankfully, kept on sleeping.

"Did you find out anything?" I asked. I tucked myself on the other end of the couch and drew my feet up onto the cushions. Once upon a time, he would have moved my feet into his lap and given them a massage.

But that was a long time ago.

Dragging a hand down his face, he stretched out his legs. "Looks like the killer came in the back door. There were puddles on the kitchen floor, leading into the bedroom where Fairlane was found."

"Forced entry?"

He shook his head. "Door could have been unlocked, though."

Or, Fairlane could have known her killer.

"Any footprints outside were covered with snow, so we don't know which direction he came from."

"Prints?" I asked.

"Still being processed."

"So you've got nothing," I said.

"Pretty much. Coroner places time of death about an hour before we found her."

"The two murders have to be connected, right?" A log shifted, creating sparks, then settled.

"We're working on that assumption, yes."

"Who're your suspects?"

He sipped his coffee. "Can't tell you that, Nina."

Damn him. "Did you check with Drunk Dave's wife at least? He said she had a temper."

"And an alibi."

"Even for Lele's murder?"

He nodded. "The day of Lele's murder, Drunk Dave's wife, Olive, was in a packed bingo hall. Dozens of people can vouch for her."

"And today?"

"She and Dave were at the hospital all afternoon. *Supposedly* he fell down the stairs right after he got home from Christmastowne. Broke his leg, needed some stitches."

"Supposedly?"

"My gut is she pushed him, but he denies it."

"Well, if she found out he was cheating, I can't really blame her. I mean, there were times when I wanted to shove you down the stairs, too."

He glanced at me, flames flickering in his green eyes. There was a sadness there I'd never really seen before. He said softly, "Are you ever going to forgive me?"

I swallowed hard. How had this conversation turned to us all of a sudden? I adjusted the blanket on my lap. "Maybe."

At one time, I would have said, "No way." But I was learning that sometimes people made mistakes. Big ones. And didn't deserve to pay for them the rest of their lives.

He sipped his coffee. "It's a start."

We sat in silence for a few moments, listening to Gracie snortle in her sleep. Finally, I said, "If you'd asked me earlier who was likely to be killed today, my answer wouldn't have been Fairlane."

"You think about these things often?" he asked, lifting an eyebrow. His lips quirked in amusement.

"More than you want to know. Anyway, I would have said Benny. Especially after what Jenny witnessed in Santa's Cottage this morning." I sipped my cooled coffee. "But that was before I realized how much she needs him alive."

I thought about Benny and Jenny's shared office and the pictures hanging there.

How clear her adoration of him had been.

How clear his adoration of himself had been.

Her future was tied to him. His money. His last name. Could she walk away from that? Would she?

I doubted it.

"What's next in the investigation?" I asked.

He pushed a hand through his hair, sending it sticking up in every direction. "We start digging deeper into Christmastowne."

"Have you checked bank statements yet? If Fairlane and Lele were blackmailing people, there would be evidence of money coming in."

"We're checking, Nina."

I sighed at the red tape of it all. He probably needed warrants.

"You'll check Jenny and Benny's accounts, too?"

"I know how to do my job."

"Just making sure," I said.

His lip twitched. "I'll question Benny and Jenny again tomorrow, then all the employees, down to the very last elf. Someone there is our killer. The motive is just a little fuzzy right now."

Why were the sisters killed? Was it because of their criminal past? Had it caught up to them? Or was it because of their current criminal activity—the thefts of the toys? The blackmail? We knew Fairlane, at least, wasn't above using it to get what she wanted.

But had she been killed for it?

Chapter Fourteen

I woke up with a start at six in the morning to find Gracie snuggled next to me on the couch. And heaven help me, I didn't mind. She was a good little dog. For someone else.

I'd been dreaming. Weird dreams. Of foot massages and dead poinsettias, of twisted metal and burned gingerbread.

Really, I had to cut back on the coffee before bed.

Rubbing my eyes disturbed Gracie, and she popped up and tucked her tail between her legs.

"Don't you dare," I said to her. I grabbed my robe and the dog and booked it to the side door. I slid the locks and pulled the door open to find a foot of snow on the other side. Shoot.

"Stay," I said, setting Gracie down in the mud room. I pulled on my boots and ventured out into the cold. Riley's snow shovel leaned against the house, and I made quick work of a four by four patch of yard for Gracie.

But when I opened the door, Gracie was gone, and a puddle was on the floor.

Maria really had to go home.

I cleaned up Gracie's mess, cleaned myself up a bit in the downstairs bathroom, and put on a pot of coffee. I brought my laptop into the kitchen, plugged it in, and sat at the counter, Googling.

The burned gingerbread part of my dream had me looking up Glory Vonderberg. I found dozens of articles about baking contests she'd won and how she was one of the best cake judges in the country. Her own website showcased her amazing talent, but said nothing about her personal life.

She wore no wedding ring, so I assumed she was single, but I couldn't be certain. I found no mention of kids or past occupations or where she had been born and raised. Was she local? How had Jenny and Benny found her in the first place?

More importantly, was it possible she'd been blackmailed by the McCorkle sisters, too?

Could she have a motive for killing them?

It seemed unlikely.

I moved on to the twisted metal part of my dream and searched for articles on Benny Christmas.

There were millions of hits, so I narrowed it down to the accident, of which there were still millions of hits.

Ugh.

Overwhelmed, I randomly clicked on links. Most were simple news stories about the accident. A few bloggers commented that Benny shouldn't have received any kind of settlement since he'd been drinking. Other bloggers disagreed, claiming the accident hadn't been his fault and he shouldn't be financially punished.

I sipped my coffee and thought about the silent victim in all this.

Carrie Hodges.

I did a quick search on her name, and only a handful of sites came up. One linked to a Facebook memorial page. I clicked on it and found myself reading through dozens of old posts from Carrie's friends. The photo in the corner was of a smiling young woman who looked to have the whole world ahead of her. Dark brown hair, vibrant blue eyes. I could easily picture her as a cheerleader.

I didn't find a single post that mentioned anything about Benny. The page was focused solely on Carrie's life—not her death. It was a moving tribute.

"Find anything?" a voice asked from behind me.

I spilled my coffee. "No, but I think I lost five years off my life. You scared the bejeebers out of me." I grabbed a paper towel and sopped up the mess.

Kevin poured himself a cup of coffee. "You should be more aware of your surroundings."

"You shouldn't sneak around." He'd spent the night on a blow-up mattress in Riley's room.

"You should eat something because you're getting snippy."

I stuck out my tongue at him.

"Mature," he said with a smile.

That was me. Nina Colette Immature Ceceri Quinn.

He nodded at the computer. "What were you looking for?"

I didn't tell him about my dream, especially the part about the foot massage. "I've been thinking about Benny's accident. Probably because Maria knew Carrie. It's amazing how one split second can change someone's life forever."

"Not just one life," Kevin said. "Many."

"True." I remembered how Maria had described Carrie's mother at her funeral and shivered again.

"I've been thinking about that accident, too," Kevin said, "and wondered if that's why Benny's a serial cheater."

"What do you mean?" I powered down my laptop and tightened the sash of my robe.

Kevin leaned against the sink. "You have this guy, big, virile, strong, outgoing, handsome. Everyone loves him, loves what he can do for them."

I nodded.

"Then he's in this accident, and he's not the same guy anymore, is he? His injuries almost killed him. He was in the hospital for weeks."

"Months," I corrected.

"Months. He can barely walk. He's weak. His strong body is atrophying."

I smiled. "Look at you using big words like 'atrophying.'"

He stuck his tongue out at me.

"Mature," I said.

"I get it from you," he threw back. Then he continued on about Benny. "He can't play football anymore. His whole life, his whole identity, was wrapped up in his career. But after the accident what does he have left?"

"Jenny?"

"Deeper than that."

I thought about it. "Money." Thanks to that settlement.

"Not really," Kevin said, "since he poured it all into Christmastowne. Deeper."

"His looks." Even though his body had been broken and battered in that accident, miraculously, his face had been unscathed.

"Right," Kevin said.

"So you're saying that these affairs are his way of proving he's still got game?"

"So to speak," Kevin said. "These women are affirming that he's still that virile guy he'd been before the accident. The affairs are about his insecurities. Young, old—it doesn't matter with him. As long as they make him feel like his old self."

I thought about all those pictures in his office. Not one, I now realized, had been taken after the accident. Looking at Kevin over the rim of my mug, I asked, "Do all guys cheat because of insecurities?"

He held my gaze for a long second. "No, some are just jerks who don't recognize how good they've got it until it's gone."

"Ah." I smiled. "That's what I thought."

"I'd hope you weren't questioning my virility."

"Or?"

"I'd have to drag you under the mistletoe and prove myself."

"Well, it's a good thing I just thought you were a jerk."

He grabbed his chest. "Ouch."

Gracie barely lifted her head off the couch as Maria came down the stairs. "What's for breakfast?"

"My manhood," Kevin said.

"Tasty." She sat next to me. "No, really. I'm starving."

I rolled my eyes. "How about pancakes?"

"Do you have low-cal syrup?"

"Do you know me at all?" I asked her.

She let out a breath. "Okay, fine. But at least tell me it's pure maple syrup."

I said nothing as I started gathering ingredients.

Maria pouted. "You're killing me, Nina."

"Join the club," Kevin said.

I glanced at him, and he was looking at me in a way that warned me to stay away from the mistletoe. Far, far away.

By eight, the sun had come out (hurrah!), the roads were still a mess, and Kevin was long gone—he'd left after the pancakes.

I was debating closing the office for the day when my cell rang. It was Jenny Christmas. Reluctantly I answered, and she got right to the point.

"Nina, I'm going to try and open Christmastowne today at two. A late start, yes, but it's better than nothing. Do you think you can finish planting the poinsettias before then?"

It was entirely doable, not that I wanted to do it. However, my good work ethic wouldn't let me turn her down. Besides, there were some things I wanted to check out at Christmastowne. Namely, the employee files. "I'll be there by ten," I said.

Which would give me enough time to wrangle a skeleton crew and then take Maria home. I dreaded having Gracie in my truck, but I dreaded the thought of Maria being stranded here another day more.

I quickly showered, folded some laundry, checked to make sure a sleeping Riley was still breathing, and made sure Maria had packed her carpetbag and was ready to go.

We'd almost made it out the door when my mother called. I scrunched my nose at the Caller ID.

"Who is it?" Maria asked.

"Mom."

"Aren't you going to answer?"

"She'll leave a message."

Maria crossed her arms. "Nina."

"You answer," I said.

"Fine." She snapped up the phone. "Hi, Mom! Good. Good! I'm fine. Nina loved her scarf. What? Yes, she found another dead body. Actually, we both did. Riley, too." Maria held the phone away from her ear, and I winced as I heard my mother screeching. Then Maria said, "Hold on, Mom."

She pushed the phone at me. "Mom wants to talk to you."

I threw my hands in the air.

"Well, she does," Maria said.

I snatched the phone. "Hi, Mom."

"Nina Colette Ceceri. You not only found another dead body, but also shared this little morbid talent of yours with your sister and my grandson?"

"I'm generous like that."

"Not amusing."

"Any new lawn ornaments?" I asked.

"Do not change the subject, *Chérie.*"

"Did I do that?" I asked, sending daggers into Maria's back as she buttoned her coat.

"Yes."

"Oh. Well, it was a reasonable question, with the Santa being on your roof and all. Is he still waving like a lunatic after all that snow? Is Rudolph's nose still blinking?"

"Like a freakin' blinking beacon."

I smiled. "That's too bad, Mom. I've got to go. I have to work."

"But Nina, how is your sister? Is she okay?"

"Has she ever been right?"

"Not amusing! What's wrong with her? Did she say?"

"Nope."

"You'll find out though, right?"

"Right."

"See if you can get her bread recipe. It was delicious."

I rolled my eyes. "I've got to go. Bye, Mom!"

I quickly hung up and looked at Maria. "You're getting coal in your stocking this year."

Chapter Fifteen

"Ho! Ho! Ho!"

I skirted the queued line and snuck into Santa's Cottage to get an up close and personal look at Mr. Cabrera as Santa. He smiled tightly as he bounced a little boy on his knee.

The boy was saying, "And some trucks, and a train, and a basketball, and a sled, and a—"

Mr. Cabrera, in a deep voice, cut him off by saying, "Smile for the camera."

The boy paused his wish-list, smiled a toothy grin, and Nancy Davidson clicked the picture. The shot was automatically uploaded to a computer station outside the cottage where the little boy's parents could buy prints.

It seemed as though—finally—Christmastowne was on its way to being a success. The doors had opened nearly an hour ago, and the village had been inundated with customers.

Whether they had come as curiosity-seekers didn't matter. The fact that they stayed and shopped was going to be this place's saving grace.

As long as nothing else bad happened.

My crew had finished just on time, and I couldn't have been prouder of them—or of the way this job turned out.

"And a new bike, and a helicopter, and—"

"Ho! Ho! Ho!" Mr. Cabrera heaved the kid off his knee. "Merry Christmas! Be a good boy!"

An elf (not Kevin, unfortunately), took the boy by the hand and led him out the door.

"And a puppy!" the boy cried over his shoulder. "Don't forget the puppy!"

Heaven help that dog.

Mr. Cabrera groaned as he stretched his legs. "When did kids get so heavy?"

"Ready for the next one?" an elf asked.

He shook his head. "Give me a minute. I've lost feeling in my feet."

I walked over to him, and he held up his hands. "Whoa, Miz Quinn. My lap can't quite handle someone of your size."

"Is that a crack about my hips?"

"You really should cut back on that cookie dough."

"You're lucky I'm still feeling sympathy for you. How's your head?"

"Did you hurt yourself, Donatelli?" Nancy asked as she adjusted her camera.

"Had a little fall," he said evasively. "But I'm just fine and dandy now."

"Like a hard candy Christmas?" I asked.

Mr. Cabrera stared blankly at me, but Nancy laughed, getting the joke.

Mr. Cabrera's Santa hat covered the patch on his scalp that had to be shaved (after doctors had to use Dawn to remove all the hair pomade) for the stitches. I'd been surprised to see him here this morning, but he claimed he was fine and was eager to get to work.

Stiffly he rose and walked slowly in circles. "I'm going to have to get some of those circulation stockings," he mumbled as he headed into the back room.

I said to Nancy, "Do you have a sec? I hoped to get a chance to talk to you."

"Me?" she said, looking a bit alarmed.

"About some cameras."

She relaxed a bit, and I wondered what had caused her anxiety in the first place. "Kevin told me about the hidden camera in here. I was wondering where I could get one. My parents are having an issue with...vandalism. I'm hoping to catch someone in the act."

Using a soft cloth, she cleaned her lens. "I have a small assortment at my farm. I'd be happy to lend you one."

"You keep them on hand?"

She smiled and deep dimples popped in her cheeks. "I get asked more often by friends about nanny cams than I like to admit. If I ever give up freelance photography, I might go into the spying business. It's where the money is."

"How much does a spy cam go for?"

"A couple of hundred."

"Whoa!"

"I know," she said. "Crazy. But I'd be happy to loan you one."

"That would be so great. Thank you. I can stop by tonight." I fished around in my backpack for a pen. "What's your addr—"

A dog yapped and a high-pitched voice said, "Neeeena! Tell this elf to let me in."

I groaned. I knew that voice. And its little dog, too.

Turning, I found Maria in the doorway with Gracie tucked into the crook of her arm. "What are you doing here?"

"Trying to get in," she said in her most condescending tone. She glared at the poor elf blocking the doorway.

"I'll be right back," Nancy murmured as I gave the okay to the elf to let Maria in.

"Really, what are you doing here?" I asked my sister.

"I wanted Gracie to get her picture taken with Santa. Look!" From inside her bag, she pulled out a tiny Santa hat with an elastic strap. One-handed, she managed to put it on Gracie's head, the strap fitting snugly beneath the dog's chin. "Isn't it the cutest?"

I had to admit, it was pretty darn cute.

Gracie, however, growled and twisted her head to try and chomp at the hat's fabric.

Maria looked at me. "She'll get used to it. Where's Santa?"

"Taking a quick break. He'll be right back."

"Who was that woman you were talking to a minute ago? She looked familiar."

"Nancy Davidson? She's the staff photographer."

"Hmm," Maria said. "I don't know that name, but her face looks familiar."

"Ho! Ho! Ho!" Mr. Cabrera exclaimed as he came back into the room.

Maria beamed so brightly she practically glowed. "It's perfect!" she cried. "You've been practicing."

He made an aw-shucks gesture. "Actually, the knock on my head makes it too painful to raise my voice too loud."

"Well, whatever works," she said. "Gracie can't wait to get her picture taken with you!"

Mr. Cabrera eyed the Chihuahua warily. The knock to his head certainly hadn't dulled his common sense.

"I don't think we do dogs," he said, settling himself in his chair.

It was probably best he didn't know the things that happened in that chair.

"What?" Maria pouted. "That's not what the lady outside told me."

"Who?" I asked.

"Green pencil skirt, black cashmere sweater, gorgeous Louboutins."

Ah. Jenny Christmas. Only Maria would describe someone based on an outfit. "Well, if she said so, then I guess it's true." I glanced at Mr. Cabrera. "My sympathies."

A flurry of jingles came through the back doorway, and I had to look twice at the person dressed as Mrs. Claus. "Mrs. Krauss?"

"That's Mrs. Claus to you," she snapped.

My jaw dropped.

Gracie growled and kept trying to tear her hat off her head.

Maria said, "Wow. You look amazing."

Brickhouse was decked out in a red velvet dress with white fur trim, a jingle bell belt, a sassy red milkmaid type hat, and a pair of tiny gold glasses.

"She looks good, don't she?" Mr. Cabrera said.

"Oh you," she said, swatting his hand away as it reached to pat her rear end.

I swear Brickhouse blushed. Blushed!

"I guess you two are back on?"

They nodded.

"I get whiplash from their relationship," Maria said to me.

"We all do." To Brickhouse, I said, "I thought you turned down the job of Mrs. Claus?"

"Someone has to protect Donatelli," she said. "People are dying left and right around here."

She had a good point.

A commotion rose outside the front door, and a flustered Jenny Christmas flew through the doorway. "What is going on in here? I've got a line back to the atrium." She looked accusingly at us.

We said nothing.

Gracie barked. The traitor.

Jenny rubbed her temples. "Where is Nancy?"

I noticed Jenny still had a wild look in her eye. Even a big crowd hadn't allayed her anxiety about Christmastowne's success. "A few minutes ago she said she'd be right back."

Brickhouse said, "I saw her heading to the restroom."

"*Ugh!*" Jenny cried and stormed out.

"She needs a chill pill," Maria said, watching her go.

"A big one," Brickhouse added.

I silently agreed, even though I knew the stress Jenny was under. I noticed the toy chest was full of donations, and I couldn't help but think about all the merchandise in Fairlane's house. Kevin had mentioned that she and Fairlee had been selling the loot online, raking in the big bucks.

Jenny came stomping back into the room. "Nancy left! She told Benny she felt sick, and she left."

"She didn't eat at the food court, did she? Because I had one of those chicken sandwiches, and it's not sitting right with me." Mr. Cabrera rubbed his stomach.

Jenny narrowed her eyes and jabbed a finger at him. "Do not even so much as hint that there's an outbreak of food poisoning here, do you hear me?"

Brickhouse stepped between them. "Don't you know it's rude to point at people? Have you no manners, Jenny Chester? Do I need to call your mother?"

For a second there, I thought Brickhouse forgot we weren't in high school anymore.

Jenny flushed and backed away. "Where am I going to find another photographer on short notice? Look at that line out there. Just look." Her face collapsed into anguish. "None of you know how to work this camera, do you?"

We all shook our heads. I said, "I know someone. He might still be hanging around."

"Anyone," she pleaded.

I made a call, begged yet another favor, and hung up. "He'll be here in a minute. You might want to look for an elf hat for him, an XXL."

"Why?" Jenny asked.

"To cover the skull tattoo. It might scare the kids."

A minute later, her eyes widened as Kit appeared in the doorway. "Who's ready to say cheese?"

Jenny said, "I'll go find that hat."

Maria plopped Gracie on Mr. Cabrera's lap and adjusted the tiny Santa hat atop the dog's head. Then she adjusted Mr. Cabrera's hat and tried to smooth down his crazy eyebrows. Frowning, she quickly gave up that task and backed away.

"Quickly, man," Mr. Cabrera said to Kit.

Gracie twisted and squirmed, trying to get the hat off her head.

"Quickly, quickly, quickly!" Mr. Cabrera cried through tightly clenched teeth.

Kit said gleefully, "Say cheese." He clicked the camera.

Just in time because Gracie snarled, then started to snortle. She tucked her tail.

"Oh no," I mumbled.

Brickhouse scooped up the dog, and I was already dreading seeing the stain on that lovely red velvet when she looked into Gracie's eyes and said firmly, "Control yourself."

Gracie blinked.

And amazingly, there was no piddle.

"How'd she do that?" Maria asked.

"No idea, but you might want to go before the magic wears off."

Maria snatched Gracie and ran.

I realized I was still holding a pen in my hand. Nancy had left before I was able to take her down her address.

As I walked through Christmastowne, I surveyed the work my crew had done. Indoor landscapes were not my specialty, but I had to admit, the village looked wonderful. There really was a lot to love, and if Christmastowne could escape the bad press of the murders and stop the troubling mishaps, I didn't doubt that it could be a success.

I followed my nose to The Gingerbread Oven. The place was packed and Glory bustled around with a smile on her face. She caught sight of me and wandered over.

"Did you need something, Nina?"

I really needed to banish the image imprinted on my brain of her with Benny, but I didn't think she could help me with that. "Just admiring your work."

"Thank you! It's a passion."

"Your family must be so proud of you."

A cloud of suspicion crossed into her eyes, and for the first time I questioned whether her ditziness was an act.

"Of course they are!"

"Do they live nearby? Will they be able to see you at work here?"

She fluffed her hair. "I'm sure they will."

A little girl tugged on Glory's skirt. "I'm done."

"Wonderful! Just wash up now, and we'll box up your house."

The little girl skipped away. "You're good with kids. Do you have any of your own?"

"Miss Glory!" a little boy called to her.

"Nina, I have to go." She scrunched up her nose. "It's been lovely talking to you."

She spun around and hurried across the room.

Was it my imagination or had she been completely evasive?

What was Glory hiding?

I stole a gumdrop on my way out and headed upstairs to the third floor. I sat on a bench and watched people pass by. I couldn't help but think about the sabotage that had been happening here. And wondered if it, too, was related to the deaths of Fairlee and Fairlane.

It would be nice if Kevin could narrow down a motive.

I kept an eye on the hallway that led to Jenny and Benny's office. I needed to have my timing right if I was going to sneak in and take a peek at the employment files.

I had seen Benny go in a few minutes ago, but he'd yet to come back out. Jenny was downstairs, supervising Santa's Cottage.

Taking out a pad of paper, I began a Christmas list as I waited. I had a few vague ideas what to get everyone, but I hadn't bought anything yet. I was a last-minute shopper to the core, but Christmas was a little less than a week away, and I was starting to get a vibration of anxiety that I wasn't going to be able to get my shopping done on time.

My pen hovered next to Riley's name. No way was he getting the brother or sister he wanted, so I was going to have to resort to video games, clothes, and gift cards. Poor kid.

My cell phone rang, and I fished around in my backpack until I found it buried at the bottom. It was Ana.

"What are you doing tonight?" she asked in a breathless whisper.

"What are you suggesting in that 1-900 tone of voice? I'm not that kind of girl."

"That's not sexy you're hearing. That's panic. I have another appointment at the tattoo parlor tonight. I need moral support."

"Don't you mean you just need support, period? For when you pass out?"

"You're so not funny."

"Why do people keep telling me that?"

"Nina!" she cried.

I spotted Benny coming out of the office. He headed toward the escalator. "Yes, I'll hold your hand."

She breathed a deep sigh. "Thank you."

Keeping an eye on Benny, I said, "Do you think you'll be up for some Christmas shopping after?"

"Will you buy me some of those little mint things from Hickory Farms?"

"Only if you'll share."

"Deal."

We set a time and hung up. I watched as Benny, a floor below, went into The Gingerbread Oven.

Hmm.

I suddenly questioned all those times Glory had been so "distracted" that her gingerbread burned, setting off the fire alarms. I'd bet my last roll of cookie dough that it hadn't been the fault of "forgetfulness," but rather horniness. No wonder Benny had always been first on the scene.

Poor Jenny.

As inconspicuously as possible, I inched my way to the office and opened the door. There was still no one working the reception area, thank goodness. I crept down the small hallway to Jenny and Benny's office. The door was wide open. Practically an invitation for a snooper like me.

I quickly crossed to a filing cabinet and started opening drawers. I found the employee files pretty fast. Thankfully, they were filed alphabetically.

I went to Glory's file first and jotted down her social security number. I was backtracking to Nancy's file to get her home address when I heard the click of the door in the reception area.

Quickly, I shut the drawer, raced over to a chair and sat down. I pretended to be working on my Christmas list when Benny walked into the room.

He stopped short when he saw me, then a smile bloomed across his face. "Well, isn't this a nice surprise. What're you doing in here, Nina?"

I jumped up. I didn't like that look in his eye. It reminded me a little too much of Kevin's this morning in the kitchen when he was eyeing the mistletoe.

"I was waiting for Jenny. I need to get Nancy Davidson's address..." I backed up as he slowly approached.

"Nancy? Why?"

"A camera," I mumbled, darting looks left and right.

"You look nervous," he said, taking another step closer. He was still smiling.

I was now pinned against the wall, nowhere to go. "I really don't like the way you're looking at me."

He laughed. "You're a very pretty woman."

"Now, see, if you'd said 'cute' I might have bought that line, but 'pretty' is stretching it."

"Your eyes," he continued on, "are like…"

"Swampland?" I provided. They were a murky green.

"Dust-covered emeralds."

Oy.

He reached out a hand to touch my cheek. I slapped it away. "I suggest you back off."

His eyes darkened, his face hardened. "Or else?"

His breath was hot against my face. Adrenaline surged, and I fought against a rising panic.

"One little kiss, and I'll let you go." It wasn't a request.

"No," I said loudly. I looked into his eyes and saw that he didn't care what I said. He was intent on getting what he wanted. My panic slowly changed into anger. Who did he think he was?

"What's going to stop me from taking one?" He moved in, his muscled arms trapping me against the wall. "Not you, surely." His hand went for my breast.

I did a little spin move Kevin had taught me years ago, elbowed Benny in the stomach, spun back and kicked him in his jingle bells. He groaned and collapsed onto his knees.

"Steel-toed boots help," I said, stepping around him. My heart pounded, and my whole body was covered in goose bumps. I wanted—I needed to get out of here.

I headed for the door and gasped when I saw Jenny standing in the doorway. Her cheeks were aflame but her eyes were blank.

"What are you doing here, Nina?" she asked.

Benny moaned and groaned.

Her tone threw me off-guard. I stammered, "I was waiting for you. I need to get Nancy's address..."

She stomped over to the filing cabinet, grabbed Nancy's folder and thrust it at me. "Go."

I took the file and ran as fast as my steel-toed boots could carry me.

Chapter Sixteen

"You kicked him in the 'nads?" Ana asked as we walked into The Ink Bottle tattoo parlor.

She said that last part just as we approached the counter. The very nice-looking young man at the counter blanched.

"Don't worry," I said to him. "I changed shoes."

He didn't look appeased.

Ana gave him her name, then picked up our conversation. "And his wife didn't do anything?"

"Nothing. And I had the feeling she'd been standing there a while, watching us. I mean, would she have stopped him if he attacked me?"

"He did attack you!" Ana said. "You should call the police."

"Technically, he didn't touch me. I did all the attacking."

"Even still," Ana said.

"I'll let Kevin know." I hated the thought that Benny might be forcing himself on women who didn't willingly return his attentions. "Maybe there's something he can do."

"Benny better buy himself a steel cup, because Kevin kicks a lot harder than you do."

As much as the thought of Kevin kicking Benny's ass appealed to me, he couldn't do it. Not without risking his job, at least.

I took a look around the tattoo shop and was surprised—in a good way. It wasn't the seedy little hidey-hole I imagined, but rather an immaculately clean salon. Beautiful artwork covered the walls, and it was brightly lit. I moseyed over to the beverage cart and poured myself a Dr Pepper. I checked for something to calm Ana's nerves, but I didn't think chamomile would work in this case. Unfortunately for her, there was no hard stuff.

"By the way," Ana said, eyeing me with a wary look.

"What?" I asked.

"What's with that scarf?"

I fingered the soft purple yarn. "Maria."

"She bought that? Doesn't seem her style."

I sat down next to her on a leather couch. "She made it."

Ana's eyes widened. "Holy shit."

"I know."

"So something is seriously wrong with her?"

"Definitely."

"You think Nate left her?"

"Only at my house last night." He was getting coal in his stocking, too. "He adores her."

"Did she lose her job?"

I frowned. Maria worked at a fancy PR firm, and now that I thought about it, she hadn't mentioned her job in a long, long time. Which was strange, because she loved her work.

My mind started whizzing. If she'd lost her job, then she and Nate lost a huge income. Would they be able to afford the McMansion? The fancy cars? Maybe that's why Maria had taken up baking and knitting—to save money. I needed to find out for sure. I'd more than willingly loan them money if it prevented Maria from learning how to sew.

A busty woman came out from a room in the back and smiled when she saw Ana. "Again?"

"I'm not going to pass out this time," Ana said, standing up.

She swayed a little bit, so I grabbed onto her elbow. She was totally going to pass out again.

Busty looked like she knew it, too, but kept the encouraging smile on her face as she led us back to a private room.

Inside, a colorful palette of ink pots sat on a rolling cart, and I tried really hard not to look at anything that resembled a needle in any way. There was a foot pedal thingy on the floor, and I realized that fed the ink into the needle.

Yikes.

Ana immediately hopped onto a table and laid facedown. She wiggled her shirt up to reveal the micro-constellation on her lower back. "Go ahead."

Busty slipped on a pair of gloves, and I took hold of Ana's hand. "So," I said, "it's a good thing I'm done working at Christmastowne, because I don't think I'm going to be allowed back."

Busty shaved the area with a fierce looking razor, then cleaned the skin with rubbing alcohol.

"Mmm-hmm." Ana's eyes were closed tight.

"Ready, Ana?" Busty asked, stretching Ana's skin.

"Sure," Ana said in a reedy voice. She squeezed my hand so tight I thought my thumb was going to break.

"Ow! Ow! Ow!" I screeched.

"Moral support!" Ana cried.

"Physical abuse," I countered.

Meanwhile, Busty had managed a curve of the heart done in a vibrant red.

Ana suddenly froze. "Oh my God, is that needle touching me? I feel it touching me! I don't feel so good."

I spared another look. "She's almost done," I lied.

And with that, Ana's hand went slack as she passed out.

"Shit," Busty said, putting aside the needle contraption aside. "She should just get a rub-on and be done with it."

"Can't you finish while she's—" I motioned to Ana, who was out cold.

"Nah. That's frowned upon."

"How about some vodka?"

Busty shook her head. "I wish. I could use a drink about now. We're not allowed to work on anyone who's clearly impaired."

"So, it's going to take a year and a half to get this tattoo done?"

She slipped off her gloves. "Thereabouts."

"Good to know." I bit my lip and looked around. "Do you sell rub-ons?"

"Your tattoo looks good," Ana said as she admired the sunburst on the back of my neck. "If only real tattoos were so easy."

The moon was high and bright as we made our way to Nancy Davidson's house, my GPS unit leading the way. The roads were still a bit of a mess, and I had my four-wheel drive activated.

Busty, at the tattoo parlor, had assured me I could remove the rub-on with a little rubbing alcohol when I was ready to take it off. I just wanted to see my mother's reaction first—a little Christmas present to myself.

"How am I ever going to get mine finished in time for Christmas?" she asked. "Think I can learn self-hypnosis in a couple of days?"

"Anything's possible. I think you just need to relax a little bit and try not to think about it."

"Needles, Nina."

She had a point. Even I, who didn't mind needles too much, had issues in that shop.

Ana adjusted the heat in the truck and leaned back on the headrest. "This present was the worst idea ever."

It certainly ranked up there with the time my dad bought my mother a new cordless screwdriver. "Don't give up yet. There has to be a way."

"Maybe if I'm medicated."

I snapped my fingers. "That's it! You need a sedative, is all."

"And I've got those laying around."

"Maybe you don't, but I know who does." And it would give me the perfect chance to show off my phony tattoo. I explained to Ana about my mother's sleep aids.

"Your mom is just full of surprises, isn't she?"

"Always."

My GPS unit told me to turn right. It was bossy like that. I had tried calling Nancy, but the call kept going to a voice mail box that hadn't been set up yet so I couldn't even leave a message. I hoped she wouldn't mind me dropping in.

I felt my tires slip a little when I crested a hill on the narrow two-lane country road.

"Whoa," Ana said. "Ice?"

Pricks of adrenaline suddenly coursed through me. I didn't know this road well, it was dark, and apparently not well-salted. My anxiety didn't ease the least little bit when I passed a small white cross on the side of the road, a Christmas wreath draped over it.

I shuddered and focused on driving, slowing to a crawl.

"Are we close?" Ana asked.

"I think the address is on this road."

My GPS chirped. "You have reached your destination."

Slowing to a stop in the middle of the road, I looked around. There was nothing but trees and road.

Ana shifted in her seat nervously. "Stupid technology. Maybe the house is up ahead?"

"What's the address again? Maybe I entered it wrong."

She took out the file Jenny had thrust at me and flipped through it. "8280 Winding Brook."

I was thankful the street was deserted as I drove on, practically leaning over the steering wheel to peer along the sides of the road looking for any sign of a driveway. I'd had to turn off the GPS since it was having a fit shouting, "Recalculating." About a mile down, I pulled up alongside a mailbox.

"4420," Ana said, a puzzled look on her face.

I drove on. The next house, another half mile down, was 3310.

"We missed it?" Ana asked.

I was starting to get a bad feeling about this. I pulled into a driveway and backed out again.

Going back the way we came, the truck slid left and right on patches of ice. I had broken out in a cold sweat. These were steep hills, some with sheer drops. "I think it's time to go home. We can Christmas shop some other time."

Ana didn't argue, which told me how nervous she was, too. She loved those little Hickory Farms mints.

Right before my turn to get back on the main road, we came across a house tucked deep in the woods. I slowed at the mailbox.

Ana said, "9873." She frowned. "That would put 8280 back at the top of the hill. There's nothing up there but trees."

"Weird." Had Nancy accidentally given the wrong address?

Or had it been done on purpose?

And if so...why?

Chapter Seventeen

I dropped off Ana and went straight home, ready for a quiet night. Riley and Kevin were back at their apartment; Maria was safely ensconced in her McMansion. Mr. Cabrera's light was on in his kitchen, and through the window, I saw him and Brickhouse dancing around. I smiled but wondered how long this "on" would last.

Down the street, police tape still fluttered in front of the McCorkle house.

A bitterly cold wind bit my ears, and I hurried up my front steps. I was pleasantly surprised to find a shipping box on my porch and hoped it was from Bobby.

However, when I picked it up, it only had my name written on the outside—not a postal address. I brought it in, kicked off my shoes, took off my coat, and unwound (and unwound) my scarf.

In the kitchen, I checked my messages. There was one from my mother, asking about Maria. One from Flash Leonard wondering if I'd heard anything about his baseball. Nothing from Bobby.

Back in the living room, I peeled back the tape on the box and peeked in warily, afraid whatever was inside might be something out of a *Godfather* movie.

Pleasantly surprised, I picked up a small plastic box. It was a motion-detecting camera. There was a note from Nancy:

Nina, so sorry I had to run out earlier—I think I caught a stomach flu. I hope it's not food poisoning.

Nancy was lucky Jenny Christmas hadn't heard her say that.

I wanted to get this camera to you, however. It's very easy to use, just follow the enclosed directions. Good luck catching your vandal. — Nancy

I was suddenly reenergized, ready to catch whoever was behind the lawn (and roof) decorations at my mother's. Within half an hour, I had quickly skimmed the directions for the camera, tested it out, and was out the door headed to my parents' house.

I drove slowly—Mr. Cabrera slowly—and by the time I'd turned onto my parents' street, the moon had slipped behind clouds.

Parking a little farther away than normal, I surveyed the house, looking for the best place to put the camera. Santa, atop the house, waved his arms frenetically as I dashed across the street. I quickly set the camera in the corner of a windowsill and propped it there with a rock.

I was walking up the front steps when the front door flew open and my mother came out in her dressing gown, waving a spatula wildly.

"Whoa!" I said, throwing my arms up to ward off an attack.

My mother pressed her hand to her chest. "I could have hurt you! A neighbor called to say she saw someone creeping around the house."

I eyed the spatula. "Were you going to flip me over?"

She hit my rear with it as I walked by. "Don't be sassy with me. Why were you creeping around the house? What are you doing here?"

"It's good to see you, too," I said.

"Answer me," my mother said, shaking the spatula.

I turned and hung my coat in the front closet and left my boots by the door.

"Nina Colette Ceceri! What is that on your neck?"

I smiled. This was the perfect diversionary tactic. "My new tattoo! Do you like it?"

"Come closer."

Shuffling closer, I barely knew what hit me when my mother smacked me on the head with the spatula. "Ow! I can't believe you hit me! Dad," I shouted, "Mom hit me!"

"He's not here."

"Oh." I pouted. Maria taught me well.

"What possessed you to get a tattoo that is so...visible? Haven't I taught you that your clothing should be able to cover the ink? Like mine," she said.

I stared at her. "What?"

"Close your mouth, *chérie*, it's most unattractive. See here."

My mother opened her robe and pulled down the edge of her silk pajama bottoms. A fleur de lis was tattooed on her hip.

I gaped some more.

My mother tapped my chin with her finger.

"Full of surprises," I murmured.

My mother beamed—she and Maria had the same smile. "Now, tell me, why were you sneaking around the house?"

"Do you like the sunburst?" I asked, sweeping aside my chin-length hair so she could get a much clearer look.

"Nina, I am no fool. Now that we're in better light, I can see it's a fake."

I tried to catch a glimpse in the hallway mirror. "How can you tell?" It looked real to me.

She motioned me into the kitchen. "The edges are peeling up. Have you been perspiring?"

I didn't mention the cold sweat. She didn't need to worry about the icy roads, especially if my dad was driving on them. "Nope," I lied. "Where's Dad?"

"We're out of coffee."

"Horror!"

Mom nodded and set a plate of cookies on the table. Chunky chocolate chip. My mouth watered. I reached for one and recoiled when my mother slapped my hand with that spatula. "Ow!"

"What were you doing prowling around the house?"

"I wasn't prowling." I examined my raw knuckles. "I was looking around to make sure no one else was prowling."

She arched a blond eyebrow. "Why are you even here?"

"I needed a fix." I snatched a cookie and nibbled.

"Of what?"

"Your sleep medicine."

"That stuff isn't good for you," she said.

"Pot, kettle," I said.

She shrugged, pulling her robe tight. "Do as I say?"

"Not to worry, anyway. The pill's not for me. It's for Ana."

My mother slipped her hand into her pocket, pulled out a prescription bottle, shook out a pill and handed it to me. Then she shook out another. "Take two."

"That's it? No questions about why Ana needs a sedative?"

"I've long thought that girl needed to be medicated."

The door connecting to the garage opened and my father came into the kitchen. He set a pound of freshly ground coffee on the counter. "Nina, what're you doing here?"

"Being surprised and abused. Mom wields a mean spatula."

He kissed my cheek. "Welcome to my club."

My mother swatted at him, and he kissed her loudly on her lips.

"That's my cue to go," I said, jumping up.

"Is that a tattoo on your neck?" Dad asked.

I nodded, hoping to get some sort of reaction out of him. "Do you like it?"

"Lovely colors," he said, reaching for a cookie. "I'll be in my den watching a documentary on Alexander the Great."

Looking between the two of them, I grabbed two cookies for the road. "I'm going home."

"You're a bad influence," Tam Oliver said to me the next morning at the office.

"I know." I blinked innocently. "Will you do it?"

Sometimes it paid to have ex-cons working for me. Tam was a whiz with computers—and knew how to get information I didn't.

"Hand it over," she said. "You'll bail me out of jail, right?"

I nodded and handed over Glory Vonderberg's social security number.

Even though she was only in her twenties, Tam looked—and acted—a lot like Queen Elizabeth. She was prim and proper, and even sat in a chair that looked a lot like a throne. Her accent, however, was more hillbilly than British.

As I headed back to my office, I turned and slowly walked back to Tam's desk. I played nervously with Sassy, her African Violet.

Tam pulled the plant away from me. "What else?"

I pulled my phone from my pocket and said, "Can you get me an address to go with a cell phone number?"

"Easily. But it will cost you."

"How much?" I asked.

"Four hours of babysitting."

That was a price I'd gladly pay. Babysitting Tam's daughter Niki was one of my joys in life. "Three?" I bartered, just so I didn't appear too easy.

"Three and a half."

"Deal."

"Done." She put her hand out for my phone and copied down Nancy Davidson's phone number. She handed it back. "Give me a few minutes."

I grabbed a cup of coffee on my way back to my office and sat down behind my desk. This time of year was notoriously slow, but the company had been staying afloat during the winter months by doing indoor landscapes. Not many, but enough to pay the bills and keep my crew employed all winter long, even though some opted to take part-time jobs as well, to supplement their income.

Including, apparently, Kit.

I'd received a call from him this morning asking for the day off so he could work at Christmastowne as Santa's photographer. Nancy was still home sick.

My cell phone rang, and I quickly answered when I saw who it was. "Good morning!"

"It is not a good morning, young lady. Not in any sense of the word 'good.'"

"Is there more than one sense of that word?"

"*Chérie*, I have a splitting headache, your father bought the wrong coffee, and there are a dozen four-foot tall plastic candles lining my driveway. Do not start with me."

"Candles?" I said, practically giddy. The camera I'd set up was at the perfect angle to capture anyone moving about the front of the house.

"They're dreadful," she cried. "When can you come and pick them up? I can't even bear going outside."

"What makes you think I want them?"

"Because you get your tacky decorating style from your father. Of course you want them."

"You're right. I want them. And I'll forgive you the tacky comment." Only because there were donuts in the office. Tam had brought them in, and there were extra glazed in the box. I was in Krispy Kreme heaven.

"When, Nina? When? I have errands to run."

"This afternoon?"

"The sooner the better," she said and hung up.

I smiled as I set my phone on my desk. I couldn't wait to see who the lawn decorator was. It was almost worth skipping out of work early.

I heard the printer working and hoped Tam had found something interesting in Glory Vonderberg's background. Something that might point to her being a murderer would be nice.

Just to see this case closed.

A second later, Tam stepped into the doorway. Creases lined her forehead as she frowned at me.

"What did you find?" I asked.

She sat in the chair opposite me and placed a sheaf of papers on my desk. Glory Vonderberg's information. I leafed through it.

"Not too much," she said. "Glory Vonderberg is an accomplished cake artist, has worked all over the world, has plenty of money in the bank, has never been sued, arrested, or filed bankruptcy."

"Married?" I asked. She certainly didn't act like it. She didn't even wear a wedding band.

"Widowed from Marco Vonderberg, the famous opera singer."

Hmm. I wondered why that hadn't shown up on my internet search. "Wasn't he like eighty years old when he died?"

Tam cringed. "Eighty-five."

"How long were they married?"

"A few years. Just long enough for Glory to be added to his will."

My eyes widened. "How'd he die?"

"Natural causes."

Darn.

"And what about that phone number?" I asked.

Tam fidgeted in her seat. She never fidgeted, so I was immediately suspicious.

"About that," she said.

"Yeah?"

"I've got nothing." She straightened my blotter and a cup of pencils. She hated the disorganization of my desk.

"What do you mean nothing?"

"The number belongs to a throw-away cell phone. One with buy-as-you-use-them minutes. No contract. No name. No address. Drug dealers use them a lot."

Nancy as a drug dealer didn't add up.

I jotted down Nancy Davidson's name on a sticky note and passed it over to Tam. "Can you do a search on this name and tell me what you find?"

"This is all you have? A name?"

I snapped my fingers. "Actually, I have more." I dug through my bag for Nancy's employment file. After pulling it out, I skimmed over Nancy's application and spotted her social security number. I handed it to Tam. "This should help."

She jumped up. "Definitely." Slyly, she looked over her shoulder as she headed for the door. "Our terms still stand?"

"Three and a half hours. Right."

She scurried out.

As I worked on invoices past-due, my cell phone rang. I rolled my eyes as I looked at the readout and answered.

"I'm dying," Maria rasped.

She sounded horrible. "Of what?"

"I think it might be food poisoning from Christmastowne."

Oh no. "What did you eat?"

"Technically?"

"Yes."

"Nothing."

I sighed.

"But I saw people eating. That counts."

"No, it doesn't."

"Okay, maybe I have the stomach flu."

Ugh. She'd spent the night in my bed! How long was the incubation period of the flu?

Suddenly I wasn't feeling so well, either. Power of suggestion, it had to be.

"Can you bring me some soup?" she said pitifully. "Nate's gone for the day."

"He's been working a lot lately."

"Overtime," she said. "Trying to earn his place at the new company."

His old job hadn't worked out so well, what with the murders and all.

"And you?" I asked, probing. In the front office, I heard the bells on the front door—someone had come in. "Did you call in sick?"

She hesitated. "No need to. I've been working from home a lot."

Hmm.

"The soup, Nina? Please?"

"Yes, yes. I'll bring you some soup." I'd run over on my lunch break.

"Chicken and rice?"

"Okay."

"And a baguette?"

"You're pushing your luck."

I hung up before she could request a full shopping run and turned my phone off because I knew she'd be calling back with more items to add to her list. Tam immediately stuck her head in the doorway. Her eyes were bright with excitement.

"What did you find?" I asked.

"It's what I didn't find," she said.

It was going to be a long day, I could tell. "What didn't you find?"

"Anything useful to you. Nancy Davidson, at least the woman who's working at Christmastowne, doesn't exist. The name and the social security number on that card belong to a local girl who died ten years ago—at the age of six."

I let that news sink in. "Nancy, the photographer, isn't who she says she is."

"Not at all."

"Then who is she?" I asked.

Tam shrugged. "I guess that's for the police to figure out."

"I suppose I should call Kevin."

"Oh," Tam said. "I don't think you need to do that."

"Why?"

"He's here."

Kevin stepped up behind Tam and gave me a finger wave.

Yep. A long day.

Chapter Eighteen

"Is that a baseball in your pocket or are you just happy to see me?" I asked. I couldn't help myself. Sue me.

Kevin grinned. "I don't think you want to go down that road."

"Maybe not. But seriously, is that a baseball?"

Reaching in his pocket, he said, "It's Flash's, from the day Fairlee was killed. I thought he might want it back."

He tossed it to me, and I barely caught it before it thunked off my collarbone. "He would." I glanced at it. It was signed with names I recognized—ball players from days gone by. "Did you...?"

"I know a few people who owe me favors. No big deal." He sat down.

I had a lump in my throat. I was *such* a sap. "Yeah, no big deal." I set the ball on my desk and said, "I'm actually glad you're here."

"You don't say."

I was grateful there was no mistletoe hanging in the office. He still had that look in his eye.

"Don't fluff your feathers quite yet. I've got news for you. About the McCorkle case."

Arching an eyebrow, he wore an amused— condescending—look on his face. "Like what?"

He hated my snooping, but he couldn't argue that I'd helped solve several murders. "Like...Glory Vonderberg's first husband died mysteriously."

Okay, so I made up that mysteriously part.

"Natural causes, Nina."

Leaning back in my chair, I eyed him. I hated being scooped. "Did you already interview her?"

"Of course."

"Had Fairlane tried to blackmail her?"

"No. She said she didn't even know Fairlane."

I found that very hard to believe. Fairlane was hard to miss.

"That's too bad," I said. "I thought we had a solid lead on our case."

Kevin said, "There is no 'our,' Nina."

I waved a hand. "Whatever. I'm as involved in this as you are. My plants were poisoned. My neighbors were murdered."

"Interesting that you put your plants first."

I shrugged. "I liked them better." I rolled Flash's ball around on my desk. "Did you find out anything with the bank statements?"

"You're not going to let this go, are you?"

"Not anytime soon."

He sighed. "There are some leads there."

Excited, I leaned forward. "Like what?"

"Let's just say a large withdrawal was taken out of one account and divided and deposited into two other accounts."

I read between the lines. Someone had paid off Fairlane and Lele, who split the money.

"But," Kevin said, "there's a discrepancy with the amounts. The deposits made into the two accounts doesn't equal the whole sum withdrawn, only two-thirds."

I put Flash's ball into my backpack. "Math gives me a headache. Can you give me the Cliffs Notes version?"

Kevin grinned. "There might be a third party involved."

"With the con?" I asked.

Kevin nodded.

"Who?"

"I'm working on it, Nina."

Patience was never one of my virtues. "Would the bank withdrawal come from someone with a last name that rhymes with isthmus?"

"Possibly." He nodded.

Ah. So, Benny had paid off the sisters.

I thought of Benny and couldn't help but shudder. I'd been doing my best to forget about how he'd trapped me in his office yesterday, but several times today I could still feel his breath on my face. Phantom breath. *Ick.*

"What?" Kevin asked.

"What, what?"

"Something's wrong."

"How can you tell?"

"Nina, I was married to you for a long time. I know when you're upset."

Hmm. I wasn't so sure about that.

"What's wrong?" he pressed.

I told him about what had happened with Benny.

"Steel toes?" He winced.

"He deserved it."

His eyes had darkened. "He deserves worse."

"What are you going to do?" I kind of wanted him to meet Benny in a dark alley, but that was just me. Nina Colette Bloodthirsty Ceceri Quinn.

"Bring him into the station. Are you willing to press charges?"

"What kind of charges? I was the one doing all the attacking."

His lip quirked. "You were defending. We can get him on a sexual battery charge, attempted at least."

"We can?"

"Nina, what he did was against the law."

I nodded. "I'll press charges, but isn't it going to turn into a he said, she said?"

"Probably. Are you ready for that?"

"There *was* a witness," I said. The office phone rang, and I heard Tam pick it up.

He sat straighter. "Who?"

"Jenny. I don't know how much she saw, but she definitely saw me take him down." I told him about finding her in the doorway.

"I'll talk to her," he said. "After all that's happened, she might be willing to testify if it gets to that point." He gazed at me. "Are you okay? Really okay?"

I thought about the panic, the adrenaline. "I'm fine, but I just keep thinking about any other women he may have cornered."

His fists clenched. "Me, too."

Tam tapped on the doorframe and stuck her head in. "Sorry to interrupt, but Bobby is on the phone. I thought you might want to take it."

I glanced at Kevin. He said, "Go ahead, take it. I'll get some coffee."

Tam said, "We've got donuts, too."

He looked back at me. "I'm not the least bit surprised by that."

I waited till they were out of sight and picked up the phone. "Bobby?"

"Hey," he said. "I tried calling your cell but it's off."

"Maria."

"No other explanation needed."

"How're you?" I asked. "How's your mom?"

"Still in the ICU, but doing a little better. The doctors say she has a good chance of pulling through, it's just going to take time."

"That's great news." I bit my lip. "Did the doctors give you any kind of timeframe?"

There was a long pause. "Months, most likely."

My heart sank. "Oh."

"That's why I'm calling. I'm," he cleared his throat, "not going to be able to make it back for Christmas. I hate to cancel our plans..."

"It's okay," I said. And it was. Really. It just...hurt a little. "Family first."

"Are you sure?"

"Definitely. I can drive down there so we can spend the holid—"

He cut me off. "I still don't think that's a good idea."

"Bobby."

He sighed. "Nina, this isn't the place for you. I'm at the hospital all day, then I'm writing at night. I'm taking care of Mom's stuff, my stuff, medical stuff, and barely eating three meals a day. Not to mention Mac and all the trouble he gets into. I'm a mess, I'm stressed, and I don't think I can add one more thing into the mix."

One more thing. Meaning me. "I think being together, no matter what we're doing is what counts, even if it's at a hospital and not a country inn." Why didn't he think so, too? We were supposed to be getting married. Didn't he understand the "for better or worse" part of the vows?

Or maybe he did. And didn't want it.

"Not here. Not like this," he said.

A heavy suffocating weight settled on my chest, and I spun my chair to look out the window. The garden behind the office was covered in snow, sparkling white in the sunshine. The tears pooling in my eyes blurred everything. "Then when?"

"I don't know," he said softly. "I'm going to rent my house to Kit. The added income will come in handy."

"You've thought a lot about this." *I* thought my heart might be breaking clear in half.

"Yes."

"And me?" I asked. "Where do I fit into your plan?"

"I don't know," he said. "I don't want to lose you."

Then why did it already feel like he'd let me go?

"But," he added quickly, "a long-distance relationship isn't fair to either of us, and the reality is that I'm going to have to be down here for months. Maybe even a year with all the rehab my mom will have to do."

A tear slid down my cheek, and I whisked it away. We had tried the long-distance thing before and it had failed miserably. My voice cracked as I said, "Since you're the one making all the decisions about our future, how about you decide what you want for certain and let me know?"

"Nina..."

I hung up. Maybe it wasn't fair of me, but if I'd stayed on the line I would have burst into tears. I kept trying to tell myself that he was under a lot of stress right now, that I should simply wait for him to have time for me—or to make time for me—that he loved me and wasn't purposefully tying to freeze me out of his life.

But...the hard knot in my stomach told me otherwise.

Either that, or *I* was coming down with the flu, too.

"Nina?"

I spun around in my chair and found Tam in the doorway, sympathy etched on her face.

"Want some chocolate?" she asked. "I've got a secret stash of Toblerone. I'll share."

I managed a smile. "No thanks."

"That bad?" she asked.

Biting my lip, I nodded.

"I'm so sorry, Nina."

"Me, too." I wiped my cheeks with the back of my hand. "Where's Kevin?" I croaked.

"He just left. He said he'd talk to you later."

"Did he hear everything?"

She nodded.

I clunked my head on my desk.

My day had gone from good to bad in the blink of an eye. It couldn't possibly get worse at this point.

The bells jingled on the front door. Tam turned to see who'd come in and then whipped back to me. "Jenny Christmas just walked in," she whispered.

I'd been wrong. It could get worse. Much worse.

Chapter Nineteen

Jenny came in, sat down, crossed her legs, adjusted her skirt, and finally looked me in the eye. "Oh my God, Nina. You look terrible. What's wrong? Are you sick? Do you have that stomach bug going around?"

I *so* wasn't in the mood. "I think it's food poisoning. I had the chicken at Christmastowne's food court yesterday. You might want to look into that."

She blanched. "You're kidding."

I shook my head. "I wish I was." I was a good liar, a skill that came in handy more often than I liked to admit. "I don't have a lot of time, Jenny. What are you doing here?"

Swallowing hard, she opened her purse and pulled out a check. "I brought the final payment for the work you did at Christmastowne."

"You could have mailed it."

"I know." She set the check on my desk and fidgeted in her seat. "There's a little extra there. A bonus of sorts, for the extra good job you did."

My nerves were raw, and I had no patience left. "Are you sure it's not a payment for me keeping quiet about Benny?"

She tipped her head and tried to look confused. "Benny?"

"About how he came after me in your office yesterday?"

"I don't know what you mean." Her cheeks turned crimson.

"Don't you, Jenny? This money isn't to buy my silence?"

Her shoulders snapped back, her eyes narrowed, and she jabbed a finger at me. "If you hadn't been in the office."

I couldn't believe she'd even tried to blame this on me. I stood up. "Get out, Jenny. Now. Any extra money in that check will be refunded to you. I've already spoken to the police about what happened yesterday, and I will press charges against Benny."

Slowly, she rose. "No one will believe you."

I guess that meant she wouldn't testify on my behalf. So much for being friends. "We'll see about that."

Jenny said, "You don't know what it's like, Nina, to live in someone else's shadow."

"Maybe not," I agreed. "But I know I certainly wouldn't cover for someone who obviously doesn't know right from wrong. Especially if I was married to him."

"Don't you judge me."

Oddly, when *she* said that phrase, it wasn't the least bit amusing.

"Judged, tried, and convicted," I snapped. "It's one thing to pretend you don't know about his many affairs. But it's quite another to witness an assault and do nothing to stop it. You're just as guilty as he is. All to protect what, Jenny? Your precious Christmastowne?"

"Go to hell, Nina. I earned Christmastowne. And I won't let you, or Benny, or anyone take it away from me. Do you understand?"

She turned and stormed out.

As I sat back down, I thought about Fairlane. If she'd go so far as to blackmail her own lover, why wouldn't she try blackmailing his wife, too? Had it been Jenny who'd paid Fairlane off?

And in return, had it been Fairlane who paid the ultimate price?

***

"I'm in a mood," I announced as Maria opened the door of her McMansion.

"Well, I'm still dying," she said, "so we make quite the pair."

"Don't get too close, then." I held out a take-out bag. In it was her soup, a baguette, and a big chocolate cookie.

Gracie raced over and sniffed my feet. I looked down at her and my eyes went wide. "What is she wearing?"

Maria closed the door behind me. "A doggy diaper."

I pressed my lips together to keep from laughing.

"What?" Maria said.

I followed her into a spacious family room. "Does it seem to you that the diaper is wearing Gracie, rather than the other way around?"

Maria stopped and studied the dog. "Maybe."

I wrinkled my nose. "What's that smell? Please don't tell me it's that diaper."

"It's lye. I made soap. Well, I tried to make soap. It didn't turn out so well."

"Two things. One, when did you start feeling sick? Because that smell is turning my stomach."

She sat on her pristine white sofa. "You might be on to something. I did start feeling sick while I was making the soap. What's the second thing?"

"Why on earth are you making your own soap? Did you lose your job? Do you need to borrow some money?" I whipped out my checkbook.

"What? No, I didn't lose my job. And I don't need your money, though, if you want to throw money at me, I wouldn't be opposed to a new handbag. The Birkin bag is on my Christmas list."

"A Birkin bag that costs, give or take, ten thousand dollars?"

"That's the one."

"That proves it. You've lost your mind." I sat next to her. "What is going on? The baking, the scarves, the soap?" I glanced at the table. Dozens of old pictures were spread out. "Don't tell me you're scrapbooking, too?"

She picked at her acrylic nails. "Nothing is going on. I'm just looking for...a hobby."

I tossed my hands in the air and fell back onto the couch. "I can't deal with this today."

Pulling her soup out of the bag, she took off the plastic top. "What's going on with you?"

"Where to start?"

"With the good stuff, of course."

"I think Bobby and I broke up."

She spilled soup on the couch. "Shit!" Dabbing the stain with a napkin, she glanced at me. "You're not kidding?"

I explained about his mother, the long-distance thing, and how he didn't want me to come down there.

Maria set her soup on the table. "I don't understand."

"Me, either."

"What if you'd been married?"

I stared at her, wondering if she was trying to make this more painful. "What do you mean?"

"What if you two were already married?" she said again. "And this had happened to his mother? Would he have divorced you? I don't think so. You two would make it work, long-distance or not."

"Yeah!" I said, feeling validated. Then I frowned. "But..."

"What?"

"It would be hard. Very hard. It would take its toll. We'd probably fight. A lot. We'd get lonely." I didn't want to think about what would happen then.

"So maybe he's doing the right thing?" Maria asked.

"If he is, why does it feel so wrong?"

"Because sometimes being right, and doing the right thing, isn't easy?"

Damn it. When did she get so wise? "This sucks."

"You want some of my cookie?"

I nodded.

She broke her cookie in half and handed it over. We nibbled in silence. I looked at the photos on the table and contemplated her scrapbooking.

A hobby, my foot.

Then I remembered when I stopped by the other day how the curtain had shifted upstairs... "I'll be right back. Just gonna freshen up."

She nodded and pulled a chunk of her baguette off to dunk in her soup.

I bypassed the downstairs bathroom.

"Nina? Where are you going?"

"Just going to use the upstairs bathroom."

She jumped up. "What? No! Don't go upstairs!"

I sprinted for the steps. She raced after me. Gracie ran around barking.

I'd almost made it to the top of the stairs when Maria grabbed my ankle. I fell to my knees. I pulled out a phrase from my past as I tried to shake her loose. "No playing on the stairs!"

It was something my mother had always yelled at us.

"Come downstairs, Nina!"

I finally freed my foot and dashed down the hallway. I pushed open the guestroom door and gasped. Tears sprang to my eyes. "Oh, Maria."

"Now you've done it, Nina!" she said, coming up behind me. "You ruined my surprise."

The room had been freshly painted a light yellow and a mural of baby ducks—maybe a scene from *Make Way for Ducklings*?—took up one whole wall. There was a rocker and a changing table and a decked-out crib. A shelf held a teddy bear, a few toy blocks, and a shiny pink piggybank.

I turned to her. "You're pregnant?"

Slowly, she nodded. "About two months. I was going to tell everyone on Christmas Eve at the big family party."

"You're two months pregnant, and you're tackling me on the stairs and using lye?"

"Sometimes I forget." She burst into tears.

I pulled her into a hug. "Why the tears?"

"I'm going to be a horrible mom!" she wailed.

"No, you're not."

"Yes, I am! I can't cook, I can't bake. I can't knit. I can't even make soap. Every kid needs to use soap! I can't even diaper a dog! How am I going to diaper a baby?"

Ah. So this was what her newfound quest for a "hobby" was about. It also explained how tired she'd been lately and why she was reluctant to get her roots done. "You can buy soap, Maria." Now that she knew where the grocery store was.

"But what about the other stuff?"

"You can learn how to cook and bake. Obviously. Mom raved about the bread you made."

She sniffled. "I bought that at a local bakery and passed it off as my own."

Of course she had. It seemed to be a family trait. "You'll learn, Maria. Being a mom isn't about cooking, or baking, or sewing. It's about love. And I have a feeling this little baby is going to have a lot of that in his or her life. Right?"

Maria nodded.

"The other day when I stopped by—were you working in here? Is that why you didn't answer the door?"

"Actually, I wasn't home. The muralist, a neighbor, was working, but I told her not to answer the door if anyone stopped by." Her eyes grew wide with excitement. "Do you know that she's the size of a grape now? And that she's starting to get ears?"

"The muralist?"

She smiled. "The baby!"

"She?" I asked, wrapping my arm around her as we headed back downstairs.

"Of course it's a she."

I smiled. I had a feeling, by sheer will, Maria would have a daughter.

And I hoped that Riley would find a new little cousin a good substitute for a sibling.

In the living room, we found Gracie chewing on the baguette. I sat down and stared at my sister. A baby. My mother was going to flip out. Flip. Out. "Are you starting a scrapbook for the baby?" I asked, nodding toward the pictures.

"I should—that's a great idea, but these photos aren't about the baby."

I picked one up. It was of a teenaged Maria cheering at a high school football game. "What're they for then?"

"I've been thinking about the woman at Christmastowne yesterday. The one you were talking to."

"Nancy?" Nancy, who wasn't Nancy at all. I'd totally forgotten to give Kevin that information. I needed to call him. "What does she have to do with this?" I held up the picture.

"See this?" She reached for a different picture. One taken at a basketball game when Maria was cheering. This one showed the squad from a different angle—it also captured some of the audience. "Look here." She pointed at a woman in the crowd.

A woman that looked a lot like Nancy Davidson.

"Nancy Davidson has a doppelganger," Maria said. "It had been driving me crazy, thinking I knew her. Then I realized how I knew her. Through cheering."

"Who is that?" I asked.

"Emily Hodges. Carrie's mom?"

My jaw dropped. Suddenly, everything made sense.

Why Nancy had suddenly become ill when Maria came into Santa's Cottage.

The sabotage at Christmastowne.

The address on her application. There had been something located on that stretch of that road...

A small white cross. The cross that probably marked the site where Carrie Hodges died.

"I'd bet you my Swiss Miss that she's not a doppelganger," I said, explaining. "Nancy is Emily. But what I'm wondering is just how far she'd take her revenge against the Christmases."

"You're not suggesting Emily is a killer, are you? Because that's crazy talk."

"No, that's logical."

Maria jumped up. "I don't believe it. I'm going to go talk to her."

"What? You can't! She might be dangerous."

"Crazy talk," she sang, headed for her coat closet. "I'm going and you can't stop me."

I ran after her. "If I can't stop you, then I'm coming with you."

Chapter Twenty

Maria remembered exactly where Carrie Hodges had lived.

I pulled my truck into the driveway of the two-story farmhouse, not too far from the crash-site where Carrie had died.

Goats played in a pen near the house, and I could hear the clucking of chickens from nearby. I wanted to go play with the goats (they were incredibly cute), but Maria pulled me along the driveway.

The front door opened long before we reached it, and Nancy—Emily—appeared in the doorway wiping her hands on a dishtowel. "Come on in, girls."

We wiped our feet on the welcome mat and followed Emily inside. A weak fire crackled in a stone hearth. Two well-worn sofas faced each other, and a large area rug covered a pine floor. There were pictures everywhere—

some of Carrie on the mantel and the walls, but on a clothesline that crisscrossed the room hung dozens of photos taken at Christmastowne. Random shots, pictures of the Christmases, of Benny and Glory, of Benny and Fairlane. Of everything.

"I'd wondered if you'd recognized me yesterday, Maria. I didn't realize the two of you were sisters—or I might not have become so friendly with you, Nina. Sit, sit."

We sat opposite her, but immediately Maria stood up and walked over to the fireplace to look at pictures of Carrie. "She was so pretty."

She was. And now that I knew the relation, I could see Carrie in her mother. The same bright eyes, the dimples.

Maria asked Emily, "Do you remember the time my cheer shorts split before a performance, and Carrie used a bobby pin and an earring to pin it until we could find a needle and thread?"

Emily smiled and nodded. "She was always an inventive girl."

"Well, she saved my butt that day. Literally."

Emily looked at me. "I suppose you figured out that I'm the one sabotaging Christmastowne."

"We guessed," I said. "But didn't know for sure."

Wringing the dishtowel for all it was worth, she said, "I couldn't let them profit from Carrie's death."

My brow crinkled. "Profit?"

Anger tinged her words. "Jenny and Benny used the settlement from the accident as a startup for the business. They don't deserve that money, and come hell or high water, I wasn't going to let their business thrive. It's blood money. My daughter's blood."

Maria sat back down, and I said, "But Emily, the insurance company wouldn't have paid if they didn't think Carrie was liable—even if it was an accident."

Emily shook her head. "Benny was drunk."

"Not legally," I said.

"Doesn't matter," she countered. "It was close to the legal limit. Enough to impair him."

"There was ice..." I said.

"There's an accident reconstructionist at the insurance company who contacted me privately with a theory. He said that there wasn't enough proof to prove his theory, but he wanted to let me know in case I wanted to pursue a civil suit privately. He was getting a lot of heat from his bosses to close the case, since Benny was so high-profile."

"What theory?" I asked.

"Based on the reconstructionist's findings, he thinks Carrie first swerved hard right onto the shoulder of the road, hit the gravel, then swerved left to keep from going off into the trees. It was then that she hit the ice and skidded across the yellow lines and into Benny's car. Why would she do that? Swerve right like that?"

"Ice?" Maria guessed.

"The road was dry where she'd first gone off."

I stared blankly. I had no idea.

"The reconstructionist said he'd seen this type of pattern before. Imagine if you're driving along and ahead you see a car coming the opposite way swerve into your lane. What do you do?"

Swerve right to avoid a collision. My eyes widened.

"Benny was drunk," Emily said again.

I said, "He crossed into Carrie's lane first?"

"I told you he was guilty," Maria said smugly.

Emily nodded. "But there wasn't enough proof. And the only person alive to tell what happened that night was the guilty party. Why would he tell the truth? He'd end up in jail on vehicular manslaughter charges. He's a liar, he's a lech, he's despicable, and he killed my daughter. He deserves every bad thing that happens to him."

"Amen," Maria breathed, sinking back onto the couch.

"It makes me sick seeing him prance around Christmastowne," Emily said, "flirting with anyone who has double X chromosomes. He thinks he's above prosecution. His ego is so large that I'm surprised it fits through the doorway. In his eyes, he does no wrong. Not when he kills someone and not when he cheats on his wife."

And not when he attacks poor landscape designers in his office, either.

Was he a narcissist? Or a sociopath?

"Did you see him cheat on Jenny?" I asked, hoping to hear what kind of information she'd dug up on Benny.

"Let me count the ways," she said. Motioning to the pictures on the clothesline, she added, "There are pictures up there of him with Fairlane, Glory, a girl from the food court, one of the elves at Santa's Cottage, and with one of the health department inspectors. He's a pig."

"A scummy, scuzzy pig," Maria added.

I agreed. "What were you planning to do with the pictures?"

She continued to wring the dishtowel. "I was hoping to see Christmastowne never open—and I hoped with all my little bits of sabotage that it wouldn't, but Jenny's a fighter. I give her credit for that."

I kept my opinion of Jenny to myself.

"She's going to be crushed when she learns about all Benny's cheating," Emily added.

I continued keeping my mouth shut about Jenny.

Instead, I said, "You set the fire in the bathroom? Cut the wires to the tree? Poisoned the poinsettias?"

"Yes, yes, and I'm really sorry."

All those plants... "Did you tamper with the security system?"

"That wasn't me." She fidgeted.

Suddenly, I wasn't sure I believed her. "Do you know who killed Lele and Fairlane?"

Blinking innocently, she shook her head. "I wish I did. Those two weren't innocent by any means, but they didn't deserve their fate."

"What do you know about them?" I asked.

"Well, I know Lele was not happy with Fairlane sleeping with Benny. She knew he played around, and she didn't want her sister getting hurt."

Ah, the sordid things happening at Christmastowne.

"And I know," she continued, "that Fairlane was perhaps the biggest narcissist I've ever met. She loved no one more than herself."

"Not even her sister?" Maria asked.

"No one," Emily said.

"Did you see Lele the morning she died?" I asked.

"Actually, I did. I saw her and Fairlane arguing in the employee locker room."

"About?"

"About Fairlane getting fired and ruining all their plans. They clammed up pretty fast when I came in."

Hmm.

"That was the last time I saw her. I was out taking pictures, trying to catch Benny in the act with one of his floozies, but I couldn't find him that morning."

"He wasn't with Glory?" He'd been with her after the fire alarm went off.

"Nope. It was the first place I checked."

"Did you see Jenny at all?"

"Not that I can recall." She stood up and walked through her clothesline photo gallery. "She's not in any of my shots from that morning. You don't think Jenny had anything to do with these murders, do you?"

"I'm not sure," I said carefully.

"Well, if you can pin it on Benny, I'd be a happy mom."

Suddenly uneasy, I said to Maria, "We should go."

Maria nodded and gave Emily a big hug.

Emily said, "I suppose you've already contacted the police about the sabotage?"

"Someone will probably be contacting you," I said. She didn't need to know I'd be calling them as soon as Maria and I drove away. It was better to let her think they'd already been notified.

She smiled. "That's okay. It'll make for a good chapter in my book."

"Your book?" I asked on the way to the door.

"My tell-all about Benny. *All-American Zero*. I will take him down one way or another. Mark my words."

We said our good-byes and walked to the truck. Maria buckled in, turned and looked at me, and said, "That last part was weird, right?"

"Oh yeah."

"I understand a mother's grief," Maria said softly, "but she seems to be taking it to the next level."

Emily had definitely taken it to the next level.

Maria threw me a look. "You don't think Emily would have killed Fairlane and Fairlee just to frame Benny, do you?"

"I thought that was crazy talk?"

"It is! Because if it's true, it would make Emily just as bad as Benny." She glanced at me. "Right?"

I drove past the little white cross on the side of the road and felt an ache in my chest. "Right."

Chapter Twenty-One

As soon as I dropped off Maria, I headed for my mother's house to pick up the plastic candles—and the motion camera.

I dialed Kevin on my way and was a bit surprised he actually answered. There was a pit in my stomach. Would he joke about what he overheard this morning? Or be nice about it? Both sounded dreadful to me.

"Nancy Davidson, or should I say Emily Hodges, just called," he said before I could even get a word out. "I don't suppose you had something to do with that?"

"Maybe a little," I said.

"She's coming in tomorrow morning for an interview."

"She has some pretty interesting things to say."

"Why do I feel like you're talking about more than the sabotage?"

I told him about Maria's and my theory.

"That's quite a leap," he said.

"Just something to look into. And here's another theory for you." I told him about Jenny's visit to my office this morning. And how I suspected that she might have been the one to pay off the sisters.

He whistled low. "That's not so much of a leap."

"You'll look into it?" I asked. Because, really, I didn't want anything else to do with Christmastowne.

"Of course," he said.

"Did you talk to Benny yet?"

"Not yet. He's been a little hard to track down. After what you just told me, I wouldn't be surprised if Jenny warned him. He might have skipped town."

"He wouldn't have," I said.

"Why not?"

"He doesn't think he did anything wrong, but I do believe Jenny might have ordered him to lie low."

"I'll keep looking, and if I don't find him soon, I'll get a warrant for his arrest. You might want to keep a low profile until I bring him in."

"Do you think he'd come after me?"

"Just be careful, Nina."

"I will." I automatically checked my rearview mirror.

"By the way..." he said.

Oh no. Oh no. Don't talk about Bobby. "Yes?" I said warily.

He cleared his throat. "I, ah..."

No, no, no!

"Got the results back from the lab on Santa's sack. It looks like it was definitely the way the killer moved Fairlee's body."

I shuddered at the thought of Fairlee's body being dragged through Christmastowne and no one noticing. "Did you talk to Drunk Dave about it yet?"

"He claims that during the timeframe when Lele was killed Jenny had taken him to a local coffee shop to sober up a bit. His costume was in the employee locker room...anyone could have borrowed it. I'm re-interviewing employees to see if anyone has any more specifics. Height, weight, that kind of thing. I doubt they will."

"Why?"

"Because everyone knew Dave as Santa. Even if they don't mean to, they'll assign his features to the mystery Santa."

I frowned as I turned onto my parents' street and pulled up in front of their house. Sure enough, a dozen candles lined the driveway. It almost made me smile. Almost.

"I don't think it's a good idea that Riley works there anymore," I said. I hated to be a bossy stepmom, but I couldn't let him go back.

"He already quit," Kevin said. "Yesterday."

"Oh! Well, good."

"Nina, about this morning..."

"I've got to go," I said. "I'm at my parents' house and about to catch a vandal."

"Do I want to know?"

"I already told you yes. But some other time." I quickly hung up.

And prayed Kevin would pretend that he hadn't heard a thing this morning. Not a single thing.

"Take them away!" my mother cried.

I'd already gathered the camera from the windowsill and slipped it into my backpack. I couldn't wait to get home and look at the images recorded.

Who would the vandal be?

Why was that person torturing my mother this way?

Was I going to turn the vandal in? Or thank him or her?

My mood was definitely lifted.

"I can only load them one at a time." The candles were deceptively heavy. "Where's Dad?"

"Shopping. He better not buy me another robe and slippers."

Uh-oh. I was going to have to rethink my mother's gifts.

I unplugged the eighth candle and loaded it into the bed of my truck.

My mother had her faux fur on, the hood up. "Now tell me, *chérie*, what have you learned about your sister?"

"Maria?"

"Do you have another?"

"Did you ever talk to Dad about a secret family?" I asked.

"Nina." She gave me the Ceceri Evil Eye.

"Maria's fine," I said, finding it hard to keep my sister's secret. I was bursting to tell my mother the news—if only to see her reaction. But it wasn't my news to tell.

"She is most definitely not fine."

"Nate's job is good, hers is secure, Gracie is being diaper-trained. She's fine."

My mother squinted at me as I loaded the tenth candle. "You're lying to me."

"Me? Lie? Never."

She gave me the Ceceri Evil Eye again. It might be a new record. I almost caved. Quickly, I grabbed the last two candles in one trip and threw them in the back of my truck.

"If I find out you've been keeping something from me..."

"Yeah, yeah," I said, jumping into my truck.

She came up to my door before I could close it and took a good look at me. "Are *you* all right?"

Not really, but I was very good at faking it. "I'm fine."

"Lies, lies, lies." She *tsk*ed and shook her head as she backed away from the truck.

I closed the door and said, "What *do* you want for Christmas?"

She smiled. "Surprise me."

Damn it.

"By the way," she said, "I do adore the antlers on your truck."

I nodded to her rooftop. "Is Santa rubbing off on you?"

"Bite your tongue."

Smiling, I drove off. Eager to see what was on that camera, I floored it all the way home.

I zoomed into my driveway, skidded my way up the slippery walkway to the front door, and didn't even take off my coat before popping the camera's disk into my laptop. I sat on the sofa, my leg bouncing, as the file loaded.

Anticipation coursed through me as the photos popped up on the screen.

My anticipation quickly turned to shock.

The vandal had first shown up at two in the morning and worked efficiently until almost three.

I kept staring at the screen, wishing I wasn't seeing what I was seeing.

I knew who the vandal was.

I still didn't know why he'd done it—though I had a good idea.

But what I really didn't know was what to do with the information.

Chapter Twenty-Two

My cell phone rang the next morning at the office as I picked through the box of day-old donuts. I grabbed a glazed and answered reluctantly when I saw it was Maria calling. I already had my fill of secrets to keep, and I was afraid one might accidentally slip out.

I thought again of the photos on that hidden camera. My shock, sometime during the night, had dissolved into amusement.

Maria said, "I was up all night, Nina."

My sister was never one to miss her beauty sleep. "Define all night."

"Okay, so I went to bed a few minutes late, but still. Think of all the growing the baby could have done during that time."

I didn't point out that the baby would grow whether Maria was asleep or not and quickly started to wonder how I was going to survive listening to these tidbits for another seven months.

"I was up late working on a scrapbook for Emily. I saw all those pictures of Carrie at her house yesterday and thought she might like to have copies of the pictures I have. Then I thought it would be the perfect time to practice scrapbooking. I want to drop it off at Emily's, but on the off-chance that she might be a psycho killer, I don't want to go alone. Will you come with me?"

I sat on the edge of my desk. It was barely eleven, and I was already exhausted. I'd finished most of my Christmas shopping with Ana last night. Then, unlike Maria, I'd actually been up all night. Thinking. Not only about what I'd seen on that hidden camera, but about what Kevin had said. How Lele had been transported in Santa's sack.

Kevin might be right—that employees would automatically think it had been Dave and give the mystery Santa his attributes, but two things had occurred to me in the wee hours.

One was that a picture never lied. And Emily Hodges had pictures galore from the morning Lele was killed. She was bound to have caught Santa in the act. Her photos might identify a killer.

And *two* was that if Jenny was sobering up Dave at a local coffee shop during that time, she couldn't have been the one dragging the sack around.

Jenny wasn't the killer.

"Nina? Are you listening to me?"

"Did you say something?" I asked.

"You're not funny."

Not this again. "Yes, I heard you. And yes, I'll go with you. There's something I want to look at in Emily's house."

"I'll pick you up in half an hour, okay?"

"What? I've got to work."

"Go home sick. Don't you know there's a stomach bug going around?"

She hung up before I could argue with her about driving. She was a notoriously bad driver, and I didn't particularly feel like getting into an accident today.

I dialed Tam's cell number.

"Are you okay?" she asked. "You didn't drown your sorrows over Bobby with tequila last night, did you? I have the best hangover recipe. Tomato juice, horseradish, a bit of—"

I cut her off. "Actually, I'd been in denial about the whole Bobby thing until you just brought it up."

"My bad."

Suddenly tequila was sounding pretty good. "I have an errand to run with Maria, and I don't know when I'll get back. Can I transfer all work calls to your house for the afternoon?"

"I'm not at home, Nina. Ian is taking Niki and me to Michigan to meet his some of his family. We're in the car on the way up there. Sorry."

"That's okay. I'll try Brickhouse." I hoped she wasn't working at Christmastowne today.

"You might want to try her at Mr. Cabrera's house. She's been spending a lot of time there."

I wished her a Merry Christmas and gave Brickhouse a call. She was, in fact, at Mr. Cabrera's.

"I'll expect overtime," she said when I explained the situation.

"Aren't you getting paid enough by Christmastowne?"

"Ach. Donatelli and I quit yesterday. The place gives me the heebie jeebies."

"Are you sure it's not because Jenny scares Mr. Cabrera?"

She clucked. "You didn't hear it from me."

I smiled. "How is he doing?"

"Alive and well."

"You know, I've been thinking."

"Dangerous."

Why did people keep saying that? "Har, har. Anyway, how long was Mr. Cabrera married before his wife passed on?"

"Forty-two years."

"Then it seems to me that it's only his dating that's cursed."

"What are you trying to say, Nina Ceceri?"

"You're a smart woman, Mrs. Krauss. You'll figure it out."

I hung up with a great gift idea for the two of them. I made a few calls and set it into motion.

I was locking up when my cell phone rang again. It was Ana.

"Tonight's the night," she said.

"It's gonna be all right?"

"What?"

Doesn't anyone listen to the radio anymore? "Rod Stewart."

"Oh. He's kind of hot for an old guy."

"You and my mother have the most interesting taste in men."

"You did not just compare me to Aunt Cel."

"My bad."

"As I was saying. Tonight's the night my tattoo gets finished. Did you get that sedative from Aunt Cel? Because I'm going to need it."

"I've got it."

"You'll come with me?"

"Will you get drunk with me afterward?"

"Will you respect me in the morning if I do?"

"Absolutely."

"Then I'm in." Maria pulled into the parking lot and honked. "I've got to go. Maria's here."

"Where are you going?"

"Hopefully not to a psycho killer's house."

"That's good to know."

"Maria's driving."

"Do not take my sedative, Nina Quinn. I need it."

My sister was a notoriously bad driver.

I smiled. "It's safe and sound in my coat pocket. I'll see you tonight." She didn't need to know that my mother had given her two. If Maria's driving was particularly bad, I might have to "borrow" one.

What Ana didn't know wouldn't hurt her—and would probably save my sanity.

I needn't have worried.

Maria had driven slowly. Turtle slow. Slower than Mr. Cabrera-in-a-school-zone slow.

All because she didn't want to jostle the baby.

I kind of wondered where that thinking had been yesterday when she'd tackled me on the stairs.

"Did you call ahead?" I asked as Maria knocked on Emily's door.

The goats in the yard made a playful *neeeeah* sound, but it didn't seem like anyone else was around. I couldn't even hear the chickens.

"I'm not a Neanderthal. Of course I called." She tapped her high-heeled boot and clutched the scrapbook (which was quite nice) in her arms.

"But?" I could tell there was one.

"She didn't answer and there was no machine." Maria rang the bell again.

After a long minute, the door swung open. "Maria! Nina. What are you doing here? Come in out of the cold. Forgive my mess." Her hair was pulled atop her head and she seemed to be covered in flour. "I'm baking bread."

It smelled heavenly. The warm doughy scent of freshly-baked bread filled the house. I breathed it in.

"Is it hard to make?" Maria asked.

"Not at all once you get the hang of it. I can show you sometime," she said.

"That'd be nice," Maria said, sitting on the sofa. As I sat next to her, she leaned in and whispered, "I hope she's not a killer."

"Yeah, let's hope." In case she was, I'd called Kevin on our way here to let him know where we were.

Just in case.

"I have to admit I'm surprised to see you both here." She tipped her head and looked at us curiously.

Maria thrust out the scrapbook. "I wanted to give this to you. I made it!"

Emily lifted the cover, and her hand flew to her mouth. "This...this is wonderful. Thank you, Maria." We sat in silence for a couple of minutes while Emily looked from page to page, tears in her eyes. "This is the best present ever. Thank you."

"You're welcome," Maria said.

"Would either of you like a drink? I have coffee, tea, brandy." She smiled. "I'm going to have a little brandy in my coffee." She disappeared into the kitchen. "I've had a hell of a morning at the police station. You wouldn't believe who was there."

Since I wasn't driving, I asked for brandy in my coffee as well. Maria sounded disappointed as she asked for water. Emily came back and set a serving tray on the coffee table. "Benny was at the police station. It looked like he was being questioned."

Maria twisted the cap off her bottle water and pouted at it.

I poured a healthy dose of brandy into my coffee. "Why?"

"I don't know. But you should have seen his face when someone told him who I was. Priceless."

I looked up at her pictures. "Do you mind if I look through these?"

"Not at all," she said. "Do you think Benny was being questioned about the murders?"

"No," I said, scanning each photo I came across.

"Then what?" Emily asked.

Shoot. It would be out soon anyway. "He kind of got a little aggressive with me in his office the other day."

"Aggressive how?" Maria asked.

"He didn't like me saying no to him."

She jumped up. "I'll kick his ass!"

I smiled. "Been there, done that. And I'm pressing charges. Unfortunately, it will be a he said, she said kind of situation. But I won't back down."

"That's terrible, Nina," Emily said. "I think, though, that I can help you."

"How?" I asked.

"There's a hidden camera in Benny's office. I'd just need to get back in to get the disk."

Maria squealed. "That's fantastic!"

I agreed. "That's some of the best news I'd heard in a while."

Except… "Do you think you can accidentally lose the footage of me going through the employee files before Benny came in?"

Emily's eyes widened. "Why were you going through the files?"

"Trying to get more information on Glory Vonderberg. Not that it helped. Turns out that other than creepy taste in men, her record is clean."

Emily smiled and said, "I'll make sure those frames on the footage are deleted."

I kept scanning pictures until I came to the morning Lele was killed. There were dozens of shots—all of which the police would probably like copies of.

Still going through the various shots, I zeroed in on one of them.

I blinked, rubbed my eyes, then blinked again. It was a picture of Santa dragging "his" sack through Christmastowne.

Only Santa wasn't a he.

It was a she.

Maybe my instincts weren't off after all. I turned around to show the photo to Emily when I heard a car coming up the driveway.

She stood and looked out the picture window. "Who could that be?"

Maria and I both took a peek.

Benny had pulled into the driveway. Glory Vonderberg sat in the passenger seat.

"What are they doing here?" Emily asked.

Nothing good, I was sure.

Through the windshield, I could see Glory and Benny talking.

"What're they saying?" I asked Maria.

"Benny just asked whose house this was and why they were here. He's worried they're going to miss their flight."

"Wow," Emily said. "You've got amazing hearing."

Maria laughed. "Lip-reading."

"Oh!" Emily smiled, then frowned. "They're skipping town?"

"Apparently," Maria said, peering out the window. "Glory just said that he didn't need to know whose house this is, and to please calm down about the flight. She said she had something to take care of and wouldn't be but five minutes."

"It probably has to do with this." I showed them the Santa picture.

"Oh my God," Emily said.

"What is that?" Maria asked.

"Proof that Glory killed Lele," I said, my pulse kicking up. I pushed my backpack and the photo into Maria's arms. "Take all this and go out the back door, hide somewhere safe, and call Kevin. My cell phone is in my purse. Stay outside, no matter what. She doesn't know you're here, and I'd like to keep it that way, understand?"

She nodded and ran for the back door.

Emily grabbed my hand. "What are we going to do?"

I jumped at the knock on the door. "We just won't answer."

"I'm okay with that," she said.

Glory knocked again. We stayed perfectly still. Then watched in horror as the doorknob turned.

Glory stuck her head in. "Hello! I thought I heard voices in here."

Emily said, "Glory! What are you doing here? Isn't this a pleasant surprise?"

Glory's eyes widened when she saw me. "Well, doesn't this save me a trip to your place? Hello, Nina."

"Hi, Glory."

That's me. Nina Colette Pretend I'm Not Scared to Death Ceceri Quinn.

Glory walked amid the pictures. "So it's true, Nancy. You're Carrie Hodges's mother. Benny said so, but I didn't quite believe him." She wrinkled her nose. "Sometimes he's not the most reliable. Should I call you Emily now?"

Emily let go of my hand and sat down. "Either one. Why don't you have a seat. We've got coffee. Freshly baked bread. Brandy."

She was stalling. I loved that about her.

Glory lifted an eyebrow. "Brandy's good." When Emily went to reach for the decanter, Glory said, "I'll get it." As she slowly poured, she added, "I think you both know why I'm here."

"Nope," I said and looked at Emily. "Do you?"

"I never did like you," Glory said to me. "A little too nosy for your own good."

Hmmph. As if this was the first time I heard that.

Glory glanced around the room, looking at pictures. While her back was turned, I very quickly dropped one of my mother's sedatives into the snifter she'd left on the table.

"When I found the hidden camera in my shop, I thought Jenny had put it there." Glory picked up her brandy and sipped. "You know, to catch me and Benny in the act. Never even suspected you, Nancy. I knew there was something off about you, and I'm really disappointed in myself. I usually recognize a good con when I see it. It takes one to know one, you see."

I silently urged her to drink the whole snifter in one big swallow. Chug-style.

"No," Emily said, "I don't see."

Glory drank a little bit more, then plucked some pictures from the clothesline. She dropped them on the table.

One was of her, one was of Lele at the reindeer kiosk, and one was of Fairlane as Mrs. Claus. "Take a good look," Glory said. "See the family resemblance?"

My eyes widened. There was a resemblance there. The hair, the eyes, the ego. Especially between Glory and Fairlane.

"My dearly departed sisters. Too bad. So sad."

Emily gasped. "Sisters?"

Why oh why hadn't I checked to see what Glory's maiden name had been? I'd bet my favorite sheep-printed pajamas that it was Walters.

"Older, of course," she said, fluffing her hair. "But I was the brains behind the business. Obviously, since they're gone, and I'm still standing here."

This explained why the payoff money had been divided into thirds. "You killed them both." I thought about making a run for it, but I couldn't leave Emily here alone.

She finished her brandy and refilled the snifter. She took the decanter and swung her arms in wide arcs, emptying the rest of the liquid onto the walls, the floors—everything. "Yes. Just like I'm going to kill the two of you." The decanter came down on Emily's head with a sickening crack of glass against bone.

Emily slumped off the sofa.

I backed away slowly, looking for anything I could use as a weapon.

There was nothing.

"If only you minded your own business, Nina," Glory said. "It wouldn't have come to this."

"How so?"

"You were snooping in Benny's office, weren't you? When you came onto him?"

"Me? Come on to him? Right."

"I never did see you as the vindictive type, though. Just because he didn't return your advances was no reason to file false charges against him."

"He attacked me."

"No," she said, shaking her head. "Benny's too sweet for that. But he's also the nervous sort and is afraid a jury won't see things his way. I don't think he'd do well in jail.

And," she laughed, "I know I wouldn't. It's best just to get rid of you once and for all. Then Benny and I will run away together. I have more than enough money to take care of us."

I prayed Maria had skipped calling Kevin altogether and dialed 911 straight off. "If you have enough money, why did you set out to con Benny?"

"Because, Nina," she said snidely, "I want to *keep* having lots of money. Thankfully, there are always plenty of marks. Foolish men." She shook her head.

She was cra-zy. I inched another step backward. I was almost flat against the wall. "Why kill your sisters?"

"Still nosy to the end." She moved closer, with nothing in her hand but the brandy snifter. "Well, I suppose I can grant you a dying wish. I made the mistake of falling for a mark. But I wasn't the only one."

"Fairlane?"

She laughed. "Hers was a bigger mistake, because only I was willing to kill for him. Though, mea culpa, I have to confess that I killed Fairlee by mistake. I thought she was Fairlane—I came up on her from behind. Not that it mattered, she still had to go—she would have known too much—but imagine my surprise when I discovered my mistake."

Nope. There was no imagining that. "Didn't Fairlane suspect you?"

"Not in the least. She thought Lele had been mugged or something. Fairlane was never one to concentrate too much on anyone else." Her eyes darkened. "Until Benny. Again, her mistake." Suddenly, her hand shot out and she doused me in the brandy. "It's your mistake, too, going after him. Sexual battery? Please. You should be flattered he found you the least bit attractive."

Dripping wet, I tried not to take offense at what she said and focused on the fact that the sedative was starting to take effect. Her words were starting to slur. I had to figure out how to get out of here. Emily was bleeding profusely on the floor, and heaven only knew where Maria was.

"Does Benny know you killed them?" I asked.

"No. Like Fairlane, he's also a little too focused on himself. But I can change him."

I glanced around. I was cornered near the fireplace. I could charge her and take her out the same way I'd done Benny. It was my only option at this point. I was just getting up the nerve when Glory grabbed a box of long stem matches from the hearth. She very carefully lit one and held it up.

She started to sing "Let it Snow," and my panic rose.

When she got to the part about the fire being delightful, she dropped the match. The brandy that she'd sprayed earlier went up in flames.

I was still dripping, and suddenly I realized why she'd soaked me. I gulped as flames licked up the walls—and dangerously close to Emily.

Swallowing hard, I fought the images that popped into my head of those charred gingerbread men I'd seen in Glory's shop.

No use. I could see them, clear as day, on a metal tray, charred almost beyond recognition. Fear swept over me, making me shiver.

"You'll warm up in a minute," Glory said. She lit another match and eyed me with a look that seared into my soul. "Your turn."

Run, run, fast as I can…

Smoke filled the air. It was now or never. If I was going down, I was taking Glory with me.

I put my head down to charge when I saw something out of the corner of my eye. I drew in a breath.

"Hey, psycho killer!" Maria shouted.

Glory turned just as Maria threw Flash's baseball at her head. The ball hit Glory in the center of her forehead and she fell with a clunk. The match she'd been holding hit the floor and flames leapt and caught on Glory's jeans.

"Grab Emily's arm," I choked out. The smoke was growing heavy as I lifted Emily's other side.

Together, Maria and I dragged Emily outside. Benny took one look at us and drove off in a flurry of tire squeals.

As I headed back into the house, Maria grabbed my arm. "You can't go in there!"

"I have to get Glory. I can't leave her in there." As much as she might deserve it, my guilt-o-meter would never allow it.

Slowly, she nodded. "I'll go, too."

"No! The baby. Stay here with Emily. Put pressure on her head wound." I could hear sirens in the distance. The police would be here in a minute. Everything would be okay.

After stripping off my soaked shirt, I dropped to my knees in the doorway. I crawled toward where Glory had fallen, but she wasn't in the spot she'd been a minute ago.

I glanced around but couldn't see much father than what was directly in front of my face. I backed out and slipped when my hand landed on a ball. Flash's baseball. Thank God it had been in my backpack.

I picked it up and was almost to the door when I saw all the pictures above my head ignite. I quickly thought of Emily and all she'd already lost. I took a deep breath, stood up, and plunged back into the house. I quickly found what I was looking for—the scrapbook Maria had made—and headed back for the door.

Woozy, I stumbled and fell to my knees. I gasped for breath that wouldn't come.

Flames danced around me, and panic beat fiercely through my veins.

"Help," I cried, though it came out in a pitiful whisper.

I tried to move forward but was frozen.

I was going to die.

A tear slid out of my eye, and I tried once again to move toward the door. I managed a few inches. If that.

I closed my eyes. I didn't want to see the flames. It was bad enough I felt the heat.

My head spun. I fought for every last breath. And just when I thought I couldn't drag another into my seared lungs, I felt a strong pair of arms wrap around me.

I opened my eyes and saw Kevin's face two inches in front of mine.

"Don't worry, Nina," he said. "I've got you."

It was the last thing I remembered before everything went dark.

Chapter Twenty-Three

Early Christmas Eve morning I was wrapping presents. Today was the big Ceceri-clan get-together at my parents' house where we would all exchange presents, eat, drink, and be merry. Well, most of us would be there. My brother Peter couldn't make it this year for Christmas, but he would be here for New Year's. Brickhouse and Mr. Cabrera couldn't make it, either, even though my mother had declared them honorary family members. They were away at a little inn in the country…

It had seemed a waste to cancel Bobby's and my nonrefundable reservation so I had given it to them. They'd been thrilled.

Also added to our honorary family member list was Kit. He would be there, along with Ana, and her new tattoo. I'd gone with her last night to finish the job—the tattoo was tiny but very pretty. The sedative plus a little numbing cream had done the trick—the cream had been the suggestion of a nurse at the hospital where I'd been treated and released after the fire.

The fire.

I closed my eyes and swallowed hard, trying not to think of what could have happened.

Trying not to think of what had actually happened.

I stuck a piece of tape on the present I was wrapping and cursed when I noticed my hair stuck to it. No one wanted my DNA as a present, I was sure. I carefully peeled the tape off and tried again.

I looked at the empty fireplace and thought a fire right now sounded nice, to chase the chill out of the air. But I could still smell smoke on my skin—phantom smoke certainly since I'd showered about twenty times in two days—and shuddered at the thought of flames. Even if they were safely contained in a hearth.

The aftermath of what had happened was still a little fuzzy, but Kevin had filled in the details while I was at the hospital. Of how Glory had been found, alive, in the backyard. She had suffered burns but would be just fine in time.

Of how Benny was found, dead, his car crashed not very far from a little white cross along the side of the road. It was believed to have been an accident...black ice.

I wasn't sure I believed that it had been an accident, and not Benny's way of finally admitting guilt.

We would never know.

Of how Emily's farmhouse had been nearly destroyed. It would take months to renovate. Months she would stay at Maria's house—after Emily was released from the hospital. Meanwhile, the goats and chickens were being cared for by Kit.

He was a man of many talents apparently.

I nearly jumped out of my skin when the doorbell rang. It was early, barely seven, and I wasn't expecting anyone. I carefully stood up as to not step on my mother's new robe. She would forgive me, especially after she found the gift certificate to the Ink Bottle in the robe's pocket and the complete DVD set of the *Sopranos* underneath it. I walked to the front window and peeked out to see who stood on the porch and felt my eyes widen.

I unlatched the locks and opened the door.

"Nice sheep," he said, referring to my sheep-printed pajamas.

Tears immediately filled my eyes.

Bobby pulled me into his arms. "I missed you."

All I could do was nod and breathe in his scent. Only, it didn't smell as familiar anymore.

When he let me go, I spotted the U-haul truck parked in his driveway.

He followed my gaze, then said softly, "I came back to pack some things up. A quick trip."

I motioned him inside and closed the door behind him. Wiping my tears away, I looked him up and down. Other than his blue eyes seeming a little tired, he looked good. His blond hair was a little blonder, he had a nice tan going, and he was as fit as ever. My gaze dropped to his feet. He wore my favorite pair of snakeskin boots.

I spoke around the huge lump in my throat. "How quick? When do you head back?"

"A few minutes."

"What?"

"I got in late yesterday and have been packing all night. I need to get back. I left Mac in charge."

He'd gotten in last night and was just now coming to see me?

I sat on the edge of the sofa and tried to blame the ache in my chest on the residual effect of the smoke inhalation I suffered. But the ache quickly spread throughout my whole body—even my nerves tingled from it.

I hadn't told him about the fire. About almost being killed. Maybe I should have—maybe it would have made him realize how close he'd come to losing me for good. Maybe it would make him realize how much he wanted me in his life, no matter what.

But he had to realize that on his own.

He had to want to make a long-distance relationship work.

We both did.

And right now, after seeing that U-haul, I began to think that he'd been right. That staying in this relationship wasn't fair to either of us.

But letting go was so very hard.

"Coffee?" I asked.

"No. Thanks." He stepped toward me. "I just wanted to see you before I left."

I nodded.

He cupped my cheek with his hand and tilted my head so I'd look at him. There were tears in his eyes, too. And that made me ache so much worse.

"This isn't goodbye forever," he said softly. "It's just goodbye for now."

I wasn't sure I believed him. A tear slid down my cheek. Then another and another. He pulled me up into his arms and kissed me.

A goodbye kiss.

Whether "for now" or "forever" remained to be seen.

"You'll keep in touch?" he said as he pulled away.

I nodded. "You?"

He nodded, too. He kissed me one more time and looked at me long and hard. "Don't put my pictures in the garbage disposal, okay?"

I wanted to smile but couldn't. Right before I'd met Bobby, I'd clogged my sink by stuffing pictures of Kevin down the drain. "I promise," I said, my voice cracking.

Standing in the doorway, I watched him walk away. He crossed the street, climbed into the U-haul, and backed out of his driveway.

He stopped for a moment in the middle of the street and looked at me, holding my gaze.

I silently begged him not to go.

He lifted his hand in a final goodbye and drove away.

Through my tears, I barely made out the taillights of the truck as it turned the corner and disappeared.

He was gone.

Santa was still on the roof.

My mother handed me a glass of champagne and sat down beside me on the loveseat. Gracie was tucked next to me on the other side, sound asleep. I could feel her rhythmic breathing patterns against my leg. I pet her head. BeBe, Kit's huge mastiff, wandered around the house, sniffing to her heart's content. Thankfully, my mother had put her good crystal pieces up, out of the way of BeBe's destructive tail.

"Do not tell your father," Mom said, "but I kind of like that Santa on the roof so I didn't put up much of a fuss about taking it down."

"Will you put it up again next year?" I asked, watching my father watch us. I winked at him. Beads of sweat popped up on his bald head.

My mother smiled. "We'll see. It certainly makes your father happy. And after the present he bought me, I can be a little less Scroogey about his choice in holiday decor."

"Mom!" Maria whined. "Can you bring me a cannoli?"

"Coming!" my mother said, jumping to attention.

Maria had finally revealed her big news. And was milking it for all it was worth.

Nate played Christmas carols on the piano as my father came over to me. "You didn't tell her, did you?"

I patted his cheek. "We had a deal, remember?"

My silence in exchange for him buying my mother a vacation to Fiji.

I added, "I always keep my end of a bargain."

"Bargain. Ha! I'll be paying for that trip for years."

I leaned in and whispered, "It'll be worth it. She actually likes the Santa."

It had been my father all along. The snow globe. The Santa and reindeer. The candles. When I confronted him, he said it was his way of taking back Christmas. I couldn't say I agreed with his methods, but I certainly couldn't blame him for resorting to them in the first place.

In addition to the Fiji tickets, I'd elicited his promise that he'd tell Mom how he felt left out during the holidays.

He said he would.

Next year.

Smart man. Maybe by then Mom would forget how mad she was.

My father wandered off to watch Riley and Kit play a game of chess. Ana curled up next to me on the loveseat and took my hand in hers. "You're breaking my heart."

"I'm okay."

"You're a big honkin' liar."

I smiled. "I know."

She squeezed my hand. "Do you want me to blow up a life-sized picture of him so we can throw darts at it?"

I blinked away sudden tears and wondered when that would stop happening. I'd been a puddle most of the day. "Thanks, but I'm not mad at him. I'm just sad."

"I know," Ana said, putting her head on my shoulder. "I know." She sighed. We sat there for a while listening to Nate's carols before she said, "It's nice that Kevin let you bring Riley over."

"Yeah." I watched him ponder a chess move. I'd been so glad when Riley had wanted to come with me tonight, even though it was Kevin's weekend to have him. It was a tradition I wasn't ready to lose just yet.

"Kit and I are ordering in Chinese food tomorrow. Why don't you come over?"

"Thanks, but I have plans."

"With?"

"Swiss Miss and Jimmy Stewart."

"Really, come over."

I shook my head.

She sighed again. "The offer stands. Well, until BeBe steals all the Chinese food leftovers."

"Thank you," I whispered.

Kit threw his hands up in defeat and Riley beamed in satisfaction. Ana left me to take him on, and Kit took her place at my side.

"Are you going to get mushy gushy on me, too?" I asked.

"I don't do mush and gush."

I smiled. A genuine smile. I really hoped things worked out between him and Ana. "Liar."

"Fine. Just don't let it get around. I have a reputation to uphold." Reaching into his fleece pullover, he pulled out a disc with a bow stuck to it. "Watch it when you get home. It's bound to cheer you up."

"What's on it?"

"You'll see." He pushed forward to lever off the loveseat, then froze and looked back at me. His eyes were shiny and bright. "If you want me to track him down and kick his ass, I will. Just let me know."

"I'll keep that in mind."

"You have my cell number."

"Yes, I do."

"Oh, and thanks again for the camera." His gaze landed on Ana. "I plan to try it out tonight." He wiggled his eyebrows.

Ugh. "Please don't make me regret the purchase." I thanked my lucky stars that I decided against a video camera for him.

He laughed and headed for the kitchen.

As soon as he left, Maria sat down next to me.

"I sense a conspiracy," I said.

She licked the cream out of one end of a cannoli. "I don't know what you're talking about."

"I haven't had a moment alone since I walked in the door."

She shrugged. "Maybe you shouldn't be alone right now. Come stay at my house tonight."

"Gracie."

"Understood. Then stay here at Mom's."

"I'll be fine," I insisted. And I would be. Some time alone wasn't a bad idea.

I hoped.

"I heard Jenny Christmas is going to try and keep Christmastowne open."

"I heard that, too," I said.

In the aftermath of what happened, Jenny had played the role of grieving widow perfectly. Benny's death had ensured Christmastowne's success. Jenny finally got what she wanted. But at what cost? I wondered.

True, she'd paid a hefty price over the years for her allegiance to her husband. It should have been punishment enough, but I couldn't help feeling she deserved something harsher. Many people had been hurt because of her choice to keep quiet.

"Emily should be released sometime tomorrow," Maria said.

"It was very nice of you to offer to let her stay at your house."

"Nice and a little self-serving," she admitted. "She's going to teach me how to cook and make soap from goat's milk!"

I smiled. Maria would always be Maria. I leaned into her. "Have I said thank you yet?"

"For what?"

"Saving my life."

"Oh, that. No, you haven't. And I've been waiting." She pouted.

I smiled, recalling our conversation in my kitchen the other day. "Thanks for not letting me die."

"Aren't you glad I never listen to you?"

"Yes, yes I am." I laughed. "You have good aim."

"I know. Was Flash happy to get his ball back?"

"He didn't even mind the soot marks."

"All's well," Maria said. "Do you want a cannoli?"

"Sure."

"Mom! Nina wants a cannoli!"

"Coming right up!" my mother yelled back.

"This pregnancy thing has some benefits," Maria said.

"Personally, I can't wait to see what it does to your hips."

Maria frowned and dropped what little was left of her cannoli on her plate. "Thanks a lot, Nina. After I went and saved your life, too."

I put my arm around her and hugged. "Merry Christmas, Maria."

"Yeah, yeah." She gave me a noisy kiss on my cheek. "To you, too."

Later that night, I'd plugged in the tree, changed into the new silk pajamas my parents had given me for Christmas (I would never be able to wear the sheep ones again), and stood staring at the fireplace.

I wasn't going to let Glory win. I cringed only a little bit when I lit the match and dropped it into the hearth. The kindling caught and soon the logs started to burn.

Feeling a sense of pride, I wiped my hands and watched the flames for a few minutes, trying to convince myself they didn't bother me.

My gaze shifted to the coffee table, to the Almond Joy bar Bobby had sent. I picked it up, my eyes watering. I didn't think I'd ever be able to eat Almond Joys again. Sighing, I brought the candy bar into the kitchen and shoved it into the nether regions of the freezer. I just couldn't bring myself to throw it away.

Not yet at least.

I popped some popcorn and pulled out the disc Kit had given me. I slipped it into my DVD player and nearly jumped out of my skin when there was a loud knock on the door.

For a second, I hoped that it was Bobby. That he'd come back.

Then a second later, I hoped it wasn't him.

It had been hard enough saying goodbye the first time.

"Ho! Ho! Ho!" someone yelled through the door.

Surely not Mr. Cabrera. He was at the love shack with Brickhouse.

I peeked out the window and nearly had a heart attack at the faces peering back at me.

"Open up, I'm freezing my jingle bells off!" Kevin yelled.

Smiling like an idiot, I pulled open the door. "Well, we wouldn't want that to happen."

Riley carried an overnight bag, and Kevin carried a pillowcase stuffed with presents.

I closed the door. "What are you two doing here?"

Riley said, "No way were we letting you be alone on Christmas." He dashed upstairs to drop off his bag.

"We?" I said.

"We." Kevin pushed a stack of Christmas movies into my hands. Everything from *Miracle on 34th Street* to *Frosty the Snowman*. "You don't mind, do you?"

Truth was, I didn't mind. At all. In fact, it might be the best present ever.

I set the movies down and walked over to the mistletoe and yanked it out of the ceiling. "Just so you don't get any ideas."

"Hey," he said. "*You're* the one that fell into my arms wearing your bra."

I stuck my tongue out at him. And was kind of glad I had been wearing a nice black lace bra the day of the fire.

"'Fess up about the mistletoe," he said. "You're afraid you won't be able to keep your hands off me."

"Keep dreaming."

He smiled, and for a second there—only a second—I forgot to ache.

Riley bounded down the steps and grabbed the remote. "What's up first?"

"Wait! That's—"

He hit play.

We all stared at the screen as "Jingle Bells" started to play.

"Is that..." Riley squinted. "Dad?"

Kit had created a movie of Kevin in his elf costume by editing pictures together in a comic slideshow.

Riley burst out laughing. Me, too. I couldn't help it, seeing Kevin in those tights and that jingle hat.

"Give me that remote," Kevin said.

Riley shook his head. "No way!"

"This isn't funny," Kevin said to me.

Tears streamed down my face. Tears of joy. "Yes, yes it is."

"Look! Dad's about to fall!"

Kevin stopped and stared at the screen. Kit has slowed the tape to show Kevin falling in slow motion. "Okay," he said, laughing. "that's kind of funny."

"Rewind," I said. "I'll make some hot chocolate and then we can watch it again."

"Do you have any of those peppermint marshmallows Grandma Cel made?" Riley asked, sitting on the couch.

"Yeah, I do." I watched as Kevin sat next to Riley and threw an arm over his shoulder. Again, there was a lump in my throat.

A happy lump this time.

As I walked into the kitchen, I pulled the mistletoe out of my pocket. Instead of throwing it away, I put it in the kitchen drawer.

One never knew when it might come in handy.

From the Desk of Nina Quinn

Holidays can be sensory overload. The sights, the sounds, the smells, the tastes, the touches. Try to take the time to simply enjoy it.

Just be careful with your favorite holiday plants—some can be poisonous and especially dangerous to small children and pets.

The poinsettia might be the most famous for being hazardous to your health, but it's not the worst offender. It is likely to cause mouth or skin irritation, or in a particularly bad reaction, vomiting. However, as I found out the hard way, holly berries, if eaten accidentally, can cause *extreme* stomach upset. Mistletoe, too, is extremely dangerous. Eating its berries can cause stomach upset, heart and breathing issues—even in extreme cases, death.

If you have a real tree, it's important that if you have pets to pick up the lost needles regularly. If a pet eats the needles, there's a chance the needle can cause serious damage in the animal's digestive tract. Best if you have pets to consider an artificial tree—there is no shame in going faux to protect the ones you love.

All in all, it is better to be safe than sorry. Choose your holiday plants wisely, keep them (especially those with berries) out of reach of small children, and if you suspect a poisoning from a holiday plant, call poison control right away.

For something a little less dangerous (except to the waistline), I suggest trying my mother's recipe for hot chocolate. Happy Holidays!

Nina Quinn

Celeste Madeline Chambeau Quinn's Hot Chocolate

2 cups whole milk

1 tsp. white sugar

1/2 tsp. vanilla extract

4 ounces semi-sweet chocolate, finely chopped

Pinch of salt

Heat milk in a pot, stirring frequently with a whisk. When steam starts to rise from the pot, whisk in sugar and vanilla. Slowly whisk in chocolate until it's fully melted, then add the pinch of salt. Heat for five minutes on low, stirring frequently so milk doesn't stick to the bottom of the pot. Serves two. Top with a dollop of whipped cream, marshmallows, or chocolate shavings.

PS from Nina: Don't tell my mom, but I use chocolate chips instead of chopping my own chocolate. If she asks, you didn't hear this tip from me.

Made in the USA
Lexington, KY
21 May 2013